Published in Nashville, Tennessee by Tommy Nelson®, a Division of Thomas Nelson, Inc. Visit us on the web at www.tommynelson.com

Tommy Nelson® books may be purchased in bulk for educational, business, fundraising, or sales promotional use. For information, please email SpecialMarkets@ThomasNelson.com.

Scripture quotations are from the *International Children's Bible®, New Century Version®:* Copyright © 1986, 1988, 1999 by Tommy Nelson®, a Division of Thomas Nelson, Inc

Creative director and series consultant: Dandi Daley Mackall
Computer programming consultant: Lucinda C. Thurman

Library of Congress Cataloging-in-Publication Data

Kinding, Tess Eileen
    Luv@First Site / written by Tess Eileen Kindig ; created by Terry Brown.
      p. cm. – (TodaysGirls.com ; 5)
    Summary: When Bren develops a crush on a new student, she lies to her friends and on a computer dating questionnaire in order to be matched with him.
    ISBN 0-8499-7582-4
    ISBN 1-4003-0759-7 (2005 edition)
    [1. Dating (Social Customs)—Fiction. 2. Computers—Fiction. 3. High schools—Fiction. 5. Schools—Fiction. 5. Christian life—Fiction.] I. Title: Love at first sight. II. Brown, Terry, 1961 – III. Title. IV. Series.

PZ7.K5663 Lu 2000
[Fic]—dc21
                                      00-032867
                                      CIP

Printed in the United States of America
05 06 07 08 09 BANTA 9 8 7 6 5 4 3 2 1

LUV@FIRST SITE

CREATED BY
Terry K. Brown

WRITTEN BY
Tess Eileen Kindig

Tommy nelson™
A Division of Thomas Nelson, Inc.
www.tommynelson.com
www.ThomasNelson.com

Web Words

2 to/too

4 for

ACK! disgusted

AIMP always in my prayers

A/S/L age/sex/location

B4 before

BBL be back later

BBS be back soon

BD big deal

BF boyfriend

BRB be right back

BTW by the way

CU see you

Cuz because

CYAL8R see you later

Dunno don't know

Enuf enough

FWIW for what it's worth

FYI for your information

G2G or **GTG** I've got to go

GF girlfriend

GR8 great

H&K hug and kiss

IC I see

IN2 into

IRL in real life

JK just kidding

JLY Jesus loves you

JMO just my opinion

K okay

Kewl cool

KOTC kiss on the cheek

L8R later

LOL laugh out loud

LTNC long time no see

LY love you

NBD no big deal

NU new/knew

NW no way

OIC oh, I see

QT cutie

RO rock on

ROFL rolling on floor laughing

RU are you

SOL sooner or later

Splain explain

SWAK sealed with a kiss

SYS see you soon

Thanx (or) **thx** thanks

TNT till next time

TTFN ta ta for now

TTYL talk to you later

U you

U NO you know

UD you'd (you would)

UR your/you're/you are

WB welcome back

WBS write back soon

WTG way to go

Y why

(Note: Remember that capitalization may vary.)

chapter.1

Bren Mickler raced to her room, tossed her shopping bags on the bed, and headed straight for her computer. She'd called an emergency chat room meeting at TodaysGirls.com, a private Web site she shared with five of her closest friends.

But now, thanks to a stop at the mall, she would be the last one to log on. Bren's friends loved to tease her mercilessly about her marathon shopping trips and how half the mall's employees knew her by name. But this time her shopping craze was justified: She was madly, passionately, dizzyingly in love with a guy who didn't even know she existed.

She clicked her Internet icon as soon as the browser popped up, and as she waited for the connection, she imagined herself casually sauntering past "him," her sandaled feet clicking across the school's tiled floor. She thought of her black beaded tank, tucked into her new white pants . . . perfect with the especially hot white leather jacket—short with a pointed collar and a smooth band at the bottom. *He will definitely notice me now,* she thought as she typed in her password and leaned impatiently closer to the screen. Amber's Thought for the Day popped up, and Bren clicked it away almost as quickly as it had appeared, mousing straight into the chat room.

I knew it, she thought, *almost everyone's already in here!* Jamie, Maya, Alex, and Amber were already online.

TX2step: Ack! Maya has 2 dates lined up for Saturday nite. QTs, both

rembrandt: No fair! 1 BF to a customer

nycbutterfly: Stop it! It's NBD. they're not really BFs-- not yet anway

Maya might be feeling casual about the guys in *her* life, but Bren was serious—and she didn't even know Romeo's name. She only knew that he'd somehow released a swarm of butterflies into her stomach yesterday afternoon.

She also knew it was bad netiquette to jump in and change the subject, but she did it anyway. She'd called this meeting to discuss the love of her life, not to marvel over Maya's latest admirers.

chicChick: 4get that BFx2 stuff! I'm in love! Need i.d. on tall Matt Damon look-alike ASAP

rembrandt: FYI u r late! Where were U? As to Damon
   clone, don't know who U mean
nycbutterfly: Me either. Where was the sighting?
chicChick: 2nd floor near gym--4th block
nycbutterfly: Sorry GF. No clue
faithful1: Don't worry. U'll have him following U around
   like a puppy. They all do.
chicChick: This 1 seems resistant. Had 2 spring 4 hot
   new outfit
nycbutterfly: LOL!!!!!!!!!
TX2step: LOL2! Make that, ROFL

Bren shook her head. Someday when she was a top designer
for DKNY or Versace, they'd be begging her for discounts. But
for now, she had to make them understand that this was no
casual crush. Never had she felt so totally overwhelmed by a guy.
It was a little scary—make that a *lot* scary—but it was also as
exhilarating as a wild ride on the dueling coasters at Six Flags.

chicChick: Help! I need advice. Will somebody please
   come over here?
nycbutterfly: No can do. Geometry calls my name
rembrandt: All right already! I'll B there b4 work. K?

Bren was glad it was Jamie who'd agreed to come over. She
loved all her friends, but she and Jamie Chandler had a special

bond. As different as they sometimes seemed, they complemented each other like French fries and ketchup.

"Well, what do you think?" Bren asked, flopping onto her bed as Jamie scrutinized the new clothes.

"Cute," Jamie answered. "But I don't see why you're so stressed. All the guys love you. We should all be so lucky. Or at least I should."

Bren stretched out on the bed and groaned. "Oh, Jamie, you don't understand. I walked right by him, and he didn't so much as glance at me. I even stopped and talked to somebody I don't even know so he could pass me. You know who I mean—that girl with the Cleopatra hair and the great big feet? She walks sort of funny— her knees go way up in the air. Kind of like a Tennessee walking horse, you know, because they put weights on their feet or something. I bet her shoes are really heavy and that's why she walks—"

"Focus, Bren," Jamie said softly. "I don't know who you're talking about."

"Yes, you do," Bren insisted. "That senior who asked me if I was adopted because she thought anybody who was half Asian had to be adopted?"

Jamie laughed and slipped the white jacket back in its bag. "I know who you mean. But let's fast-forward, okay? If I'm late for work, Mr. Cross will have my neck. He got a new deep fryer, and we all have to be there early for one of his training sessions."

Bren sat up. "Okay! Okay! The thing is, even after I gave him a second chance, he looked right through me. You'd have thought I was a ghost! Did you ever see *Casper?* It was really for little kids I guess, but—"

"Why didn't you just say 'hi' to him?" Jamie asked, interrupting the digression. "Wouldn't that have been easier than all this shopping and agonizing?"

"No waaaaaaaay!" Bren moaned. She stood up and rummaged through the plastic container she used to store her makeup. "Which of these do you like better?" She held out a tube of chocolate lipstick and a small silver container of something called Lip Shine.

"If that's gloss, I vote for that," Jamie replied pointing to the silver disk. "You don't want to be too obvious."

The next morning, Bren arrived at school early, her lips slicked with the rose gloss, hoping to spot Romeo before first block while she still looked her absolute best. But he was nowhere to be found. At lunch she took out her black wire-frame glasses, perched them low on her nose, and scanned the crowded lunchroom. Again, nothing. Either Romeo didn't have her lunch period, or he was on a starvation diet.

By the time the bell rang signaling the end of third block, she felt like she was going into an auto self-destruct mode, imminent implosion at any moment. If she didn't see him now, well then, he must have been a figment of her imagination. Her heart pounded as she retraced yesterday's steps toward the gym.

"Hey Bren!" a voice called behind her in the hall. Bren turned and spotted Amber Thomas, her right hand waving above the throng of students' heads.

"Come here a sec!"

Bren nudged her way toward Amber, who not only swam her team's best backstroke but created most of their Web site all by herself. Bren glanced nervously around the hall as she shuffled through, not wanting to miss Romeo.

"What's up?" Bren asked, glancing at Amber and then scanning the sea of bodies surging in both directions.

"Coach Short left this note on my locker," Amber said, holding it out so Bren could see. "He wants you at swim practice next time. No excuses."

"Sure. Whatever." Bren's well-manicured hands folded the paper and stuffed it into her bag. "Listen, I gotta run. I'll catch up with you later, okay?" What difference did it make if she showed up at swim practice? It's not like she was *really* on the roster. The only reason she swam at all was to hang out with her friends. She wasn't a strong enough swimmer to compete in meets.

Bren rejoined the river of bodies moving down the hall. She craned her neck to spot a tall blond head looming over the crowd. At first she didn't see him and then—all of a sudden—there he was! Maneuvering her way through a clutch of giggling freshmen, she positioned herself behind his broad shoulders. For a few seconds she walked behind him, then tucked her shoulder-length hair behind one ear, and casually passed him. At the gym doors, she stopped and pretended to look for something in her bag.

"Ha-ha! Like I care, man!" a male voice rumbled. She looked toward its owner and saw Romeo jab at one of his noisy buddies, almost connecting with the Cleopatra girl instead. "Sorry!" he muttered, jumping back. The heel of his giant sneaker crashed down on Bren's pink toenails.

"Owwwwwwwwwwwwwww!"

The pain almost left her breathless. She instinctively reached down to massage her wounded digits, sending her shoulder bag crashing to the crook of her arm. She watched in horror as it executed a perfect forward flip and rained makeup, pens, coins, hair clips, and Kleenex all over the floor. Bren dived to the ground, wishing she would turn into Casper again.

"I think you dropped this," she heard from somewhere up in the stratosphere.

Bren looked up. Romeo held out the small fuzzy red Elmo doll her father had given her for Christmas! Nobody—not even the TodaysGirls—knew that she and her dad still watched *Sesame Street* together. Bren managed a weak smile, snatched up the doll, shoved it into her bag, and ran, leaving a pile of tissues and a couple of pens lying in the hall. By the time she fell into her desk in math, she felt like she'd just escaped a kidnapper.

She spent the rest of the block planning her transfer to St. Bridget's Academy for Girls.

After the final bell, Bren gathered up her books and went to her locker. She looked around for Jamie, then remembered that she was riding with Maya to the Gnosh Pit, the fifties-style diner where they often worked after school and on weekends. Maya and Morgan's dad owned the Gnosh, and Maya gave Jamie a ride sometimes, especially when they were both working.

Bren traded two of the books in her arms for the poetry book they'd begin tomorrow in English Lit. Then she slammed the door of her locker and headed out into the cool, early spring air. She wanted to get home but felt guilty about brushing Amber off earlier. She decided to wait by the side door near the swim team office where Amber was no doubt reporting to Coach Short that her mission was accomplished: Bren Mickler would duly report for swim practice.

"Yeah, later, Charlie!" a now-familiar voice called.

Bren felt her pulse quicken. She looked up just as Romeo emerged from the side door of the school. He glanced at her, then tapped his bare wrist.

"Hey, you got the time?" he asked her. "I forgot my watch."

Bren looked at her own wrist. She'd been so busy searching for her onyx studs this morning she'd forgotten her watch, too. She shook her head no, mumbled, "sorry," and pretended to be busy examining the new poetry book. Out of the corner of her eye, she could see him pacing back and forth like he was waiting for someone to pick him up.

This is your chance! she thought. *Don't blow it. Do something, for heaven's sake!*

The small, insistent voice screamed inside her head. She glanced up and thought for a second. After what happened this afternoon, he probably thought she belonged back in middle school. What could she do to convince him that nothing could be farther from the truth? No way did she want to talk to him. It would be way too obvious. Much better to pretend like he didn't exist.

Bren reached into her bag and pulled out the cell phone her parents insisted she carry for emergencies. She held it to her ear and waited a second before letting out a little yelp of surprise.

"Oh! It never even rang!" she said into the empty phone. "I was just about to dial out. What's up?"

She waited for what she thought was enough time for her "caller" to say something.

"Really?" she said. "Well, I don't know if I can do it THAT fast. I have a design on the table right now. By the time I finish it and make a prototype . . . " She allowed her voice to drift off in a noncommittal cloud and sneaked a peek at Romeo.

It was hard to tell whether or not he was listening. He was still pacing and looking up the street toward the center of town.

"The new design? Oh, it's a commission piece. A prom dress." She hoped the word *prom* jingled a bell in his brain. "Yes, prom," she repeated, feeling braver. "A sheath—black with jet beads on the bodice."

She caught herself before she launched a full description of the dress. Until this second, it hadn't even existed in her mind.

"Well, let me think about it and get back to you, okay? Okay. *Ciao.*"

The last word was a touch of genius, she thought, as she shoved the phone back in her purse. She had absolutely no idea where it came from. Even the most sophisticated people in Edgewood, Indiana, didn't run around saying things like *ciao.*

Romeo glanced over at her and sort of smiled. Or maybe smiled. It might actually have been a smirk. Bren couldn't tell for sure. Just then a dark green Jeep Cherokee glided to the curb. She watched him climb in, and she noticed the casual way he carried himself. He started to slam the door, then looked over at her.

"Hey! I've got a tip for you," he called. "Next time you use your cell phone, press the 'on' button. I hear it works better."

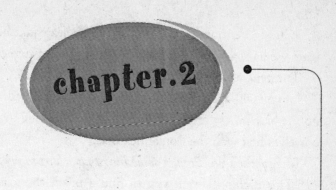

chapter.2

"I am sooooo mortified," Bren told Jamie for the twenty-seventh time since yesterday afternoon. "Why did I do it? What was I thinking?"

Jamie grinned. "Thinking had nothing to do with it, girl-friend."

The girls were in English, waiting for the bell to signal the start of class. They had a sub for the next six weeks while their regular teacher taught a portfolio conference in San Diego. With any luck, her replacement wouldn't pile on the homework.

"He's sort of handsome for an old guy, isn't he?" Jamie whispered, referring to J.W. Bailey, the tall, bearded teacher at the front of the room.

"Hmmm? Oh, him." Bren shrugged. "He looks like he ought to be a college professor."

"Class! Attention, please! Will everyone please take his or her seat? We have a lot of ground to cover," the substitute called.

The general roar softened to a mild rustle.

"If you will open to the first chapter," he continued, holding up the blue poetry text, "you'll see that we are going to concern ourselves first with the Romantic poets."

Bren perked up. *Finally, something that relates to my life!*

"This evening I want you to find a poem about love that appeals to you. It doesn't have to come from the text—the Romantics didn't write only of love. Just choose a piece that strikes a chord. It can be either old or contemporary, and the author can be either famous or infamous." Here he paused to offer a ghost of a smile only understood by Bren and a few people sitting in front of her on the first row.

"The important thing," the sub continued, "is that it holds meaning for you. I want you to write an essay—five-hundred words—on what you think the poet was trying to say and how his or her message speaks directly to your life."

Bren sighed. Lines from old poems rattled around in her brain like loose beads. She loved Elizabeth Barrett Browning, but everybody would choose "How Do I Love Thee?" from *Sonnets from the Portuguese.* There was another old poem she liked by Mathew Arnold—something about unspoken love. Bren smiled, remembering the lines she'd read in an old book of her father's while she was waiting for him to get off the phone. For some reason one part in particular had stuck in her head.

"Do you know what you're going to pick?" she whispered to Jamie. "I think I've got mine. I LOVE old poetry. It's way more romantic than the stuff they write now."

"No clue what I'll choose," Jamie hissed back. "This old stuff doesn't do it for me. I like poetry best when it's lyrics on the radio."

Mr. J.W. Bailey raised his eyebrows and stroked his beard. "There seems to be an inordinate amount of interest in the second row," he said, looking pointedly at Bren and Jamie. "You two clearly want to be first tomorrow."

Jamie blushed, but Bren was only too happy to read her poem first. It was over a hundred years old, but it zeroed right in on the absolute awfulness of falling in love. And the best part was that she'd found it with no effort.

After class the girls walked in the hall together. "Something weird is going on with my mom," Jamie confided as they joined the stampeding mob changing classes.

Bren had been struggling to remember the name of her poem, but this news brought her attention back to her best friend. Jamie's mom was single, raising Jamie and her sisters, Jessica and Jordan, on her salary as a paralegal. They weren't poor, but Bren knew that the Chandlers' reality was a far cry from the life she and her family took for granted.

"What's wrong? She's not sick or anything, is she?"

Jamie shook her head. "No, no, nothing like that. It's more the way she's been acting lately. It's like she's not there. Last night

Jessica had the TV so loud it would have blasted a man to the moon, and it was like Mom never even heard it. Then Jordan and I got into a fight over the last Sprite, and Mom didn't say a word. Her eyes were all faraway looking, and she just smiled at us like she was on something. I don't get it."

Bren let out a squeal. "Maybe she's in love, Jamie!"

Jamie shook her head. "Hardly. She's always either working or going to night class—when would she have time to go on a date? And who would ask her out anyway? Something's totally wrong with her, and I don't know what's up at all!"

"I'm telling you, Jamie, it's love," Bren said lightly. "Listen—not to change the subject—but what should I do about Romeo? I've got to find out who he is."

"Him again?" Jamie rolled her eyes. "If you had any sense, you'd leave it alone. But I know you won't. You're gonna go off about this until you figure out who he is, aren't you?"

"Yup, I sure will," Bren said cheerfully.

Jamie sighed. "Okay then, come over tonight before I go to the Gnosh. We'll get Martin from the yearbook staff to send us his database files. If we can somehow narrow down the entire Edgewood High student body, we can run a people search on the most likely candidates."

Bren's brown eyes lit up. "Cool! Why didn't I think of that? Tell you what—you help me with the people search thing, and I'll help you with the poem. Deal?"

"Deal," Jamie agreed.

After school, Bren walked the short distance with Jamie to the Chandlers' house on Cedar Street. Jamie fumbled for her keys as they walked up the porch steps, and Bren noticed something on the front door. A piece of VeggieTales stationery was taped waist-high to the storm-door glass. Jamie glanced up, then at Bren, and they both knew exactly who left the note: Jamie's sister, Jessica, the world's most responsible nine-year-old, who constantly left instructional memos all over the house. Jamie pulled the note from the door.

"Says the munchkins are riding with Mom today . . . home later than usual!" Jamie smiled, unlocking the door. "We've got the house to ourselves!"

"How could you forget?" Bren asked as they walked into the living room. "It's never this quiet. Kinda creepy, huh?" Bren followed Jamie to the kitchen, where they grabbed an extra chair and some chips to munch during their detective work.

In Jamie's room, they hunched over the slow, older model computer. Jamie had e-mailed Martin at the yearbook office from school, and he had already replied with a complete listing of all the students at Edgewood High School.

"Look here," Jamie said, pointing to an asterisk by a name on the first screen. "An asterisk denotes new people. I think your mystery man must be new, don't you? Otherwise one of us would already know who he is. This'll be a piece of cake."

Bren squirmed in the kitchen chair they'd dragged into Jamie's room. She couldn't wait to find out Romeo's identity.

"Okay, get a pen and jot down the names as I say 'em," Jamie ordered. "We'll just copy the boys with asterisks beside them." Jamie quickly scrolled down the huge list of names. When she reached the bottom, they wound up with only two possibilities—Christopher Russell and Brian Watson.

"Mmmmm, Bren Rhiannon Russell. Or Bren Rhiannon Watson," Bren murmured dreamily. "Hi, I'm Bren Russell. Yes, I am Bren Watson. Which one sounds best, Jamie?"

Jamie grabbed the paper with the two names from her friend's hand, rolled it up like a newspaper, and bopped Bren on the head with it. "Hello! We still have to do the people search, remember?"

Bren climbed off her rosy cloud and watched as Jamie typed into the address box at the top of her browser. When the search engine came up, they looked to the sidebar on the right, and Jamie clicked on People Search. "The problem is, both Russell and Watson are pretty common names," she mused.

When the Go People Search screen loaded, Jamie skipped past the box that said First Name and typed "Russell" in the Last Name box next to it. Then she typed in the city and pulled down the little menu box, scrolling until she reached Indiana. One click on the state abbreviation and a keypunch to *Enter,* and they had it. Four possibilities popped up.

"Look!" Bren squealed over Jamie's shoulder. "One says Christopher! Maybe it's his dad."

Jamie frowned and leaned forward, studying the four

choices. "I don't think so," she said, tapping the glass with her pen. "Look here. There's a James P. Russell at the same address on Crocus Drive. Looks like our boy Christopher has his own phone."

"Click on the map," Bren suggested. "I don't recognize the street. It must be in one of the new developments. Then print it out for me, okay?"

Jamie did as instructed. While the ancient printer chugged out the map, Bren had a brain-flash. "E-mail Maya for me too! I know you have to get to the Gnosh, but if she's not working tonight, maybe she'll drive around with me and find where these guys live."

"Alright, but let's do my poem first," Jamie said, dashing off a quick note to Maya, while Bren watched over her shoulder. They repeated the same process for Watson with People Search. This time eight possibilities presented themselves.

"Forget these three," Jamie said. "And that one and that one. All of them are out in the country—too far to be Edgewood High. That leaves us with Baxter Street and New Meadow Drive. You don't need a map for these, so I'll just print the list, and you can go visit them." She hit *Print* and turned around in her chair. "Okay, now—give. What's my poem?"

Bren leaned back in her chair and closed her eyes, "'Shall I compare thee to a summer's day?'" she recited. "'Thou art more lovely and more temperate . . .'"

"STOP!" Jamie cried, clamping both hands over her ears.

"There is no way I'm reading *that*. No way! How does that relate directly to my life?"

"It's Shakespeare," Bren said. "It's beautiful, romantic, and all about love." Bren stood up in the kitchen chair, raising her arms above her head. "You *make* it relate to your life. It becomes part of your very essence," she cried.

"Whatever. It's sappy," Jamie protested. "Now get down before you hurt yourself."

Bren looked down sheepishly from her self-made soapbox with her arms still raised. Suddenly they heard what sounded like a small invasion at the front of the house.

"Thank God," Jamie said. "I'm going to go ask my mother. *She* at least is a sensible person."

Bren followed her into the kitchen of the small ranch house. Jamie's mom was depositing an armload of paperwork and a supersized PizzaMan pizza on the kitchen table. Bren could tell she'd picked up the girls straight from the office, because she was still dressed in a gray business suit. Jessica and Jordan were dragging in groceries from the car.

"Mom?" Jamie said. "I know you're tired and busy, but I need a poem about love by tomorrow. This new sub Mr. Bailey—he's majorly weird—wants us to relate it *directly* to our lives." She stuck her hand into a grocery bag and grabbed a yogurt to take with her to the Gnosh for a snack during her break.

"Oh, cut the poor guy some slack, Jamie," Ms. Chandler sighed, putting a carton of milk in the fridge. "Most of the time, you two complain that what you learn has nothing to do with the real world. Be glad he's trying to make this class relevant."

Jamie shrugged. "So what do you think?" she pressed. "Do you have any ideas?"

"I tried to give her a Shakespearean sonnet," Bren offered. "But she turned me down flat."

"I have just the thing," Ms. Chandler said, closing the refrigerator door and starting across the kitchen, only to halt abruptly at the ringing phone, which she snagged with the urgency of a shortstop in mid-play.

"Hello?" she cooed.

Bren and Jamie looked at each other with furrowed brows— Jamie's mom rarely cooed.

"Now why would you say that?" Ms. Chandler asked with a soft, musical little giggle.

Bren gave Jamie a nudge with her elbow. Jamie returned the nudge with a frown.

"Mom?" she asked quietly, going over to her.

Jamie's mom looked up at her daughter and held up an index finger. "I've got to run, Jack," she said into the phone. "My first-born needs me. I'll give some thought to what you suggested though. It could work."

Bren's dark eyes danced. Jamie shook her head no. "Business," she mouthed, her back to her mother.

Ms. Chandler hung up the receiver and went over to a small wicker basket hanging next to the wooden door leading out to the garage. She rifled through it and pulled out a tasseled book-mark. "This isn't exactly a poem," she said. "But the words are certainly as beautiful as one. In my book, it's the truest thing about love ever written."

Jamie took the bookmark and read aloud from 1 Corinthians 13:4–8, "'Love is patient and kind. Love is not jealous, it does not brag, and it is not proud. Love is not rude, is not selfish, and does not become angry easily. Love does not remember wrongs done against it. Love is not happy with evil, but is happy with the truth. Love patiently accepts all things. It always trusts, always hopes, and always continues strong. Love never ends.'"

"Patient and kind . . . always strong," Bren repeated dream-ily. "That's so romantic."

"I like it too, but I don't think it's about romance," Jamie said. "Thanks, Mom."

Outside, the unmistakable *beeeeeep-beeeeep* of Maya Cross's car horn sounded in the driveway. "Gotta go!" Jamie cried, planting a kiss on her mother's cheek.

Jamie dropped the bookmark back in the basket for later, grabbed her yogurt, and headed outside with Bren in tow.

"Thanks," Bren called over her shoulder. "See ya later!"

Jamie's little sisters stood by the passenger seat window, jab-bering excitedly with Maya's younger sister, Morgan. Shooing the pair back to their grocery duties, Bren and Jamie scrunched into the VW Beetle's tiny backseat. Already sitting behind Maya was Morgan's best friend, Alex. She scooted as far left as possible while the girls layered themselves into the car and struggled with the too-tight safety belts Mr. Cross had installed himself.

"Hi, hi, hi," Bren greeted everyone. "Thanks for doing this, Maya. You're saving my life."

In the rearview mirror, Maya's brown eyes sparkled. "You're nothing if not dramatic, Bren," she laughed. She shifted gears and guided the small car she called Mr. Beep out of the drive and onto Cedar toward the Gnosh.

When they'd dropped Jamie off at work, Maya turned around and looked at Bren. "So where we headed next?" she asked.

Bren handed over the lists of Russells and Watsons and the map to the home of James P. and Christopher Russell on Crocus Drive. "We have him narrowed down to either Brian Watson or Christopher Russell," she explained.

Maya handed back the page of Watsons. "I can tell you right now—this one's not your man," she said. "I know Brian Watson. Cute, but not the type you described. He's a jock, but also a serious student and very quiet. Nice too. He'd never say anything about the cell phone like your Mr. Wonderful did."

Bren crumpled up the page of Watsons and ignored the sarcasm. Maya didn't know Romeo. She had no clue what she was talking about. The only reason he'd embarrassed her like that was because he was so cool that he couldn't help himself. Cool people simply didn't do dorky things like conduct imaginary conversations on cell phones. And they couldn't stand it when *normally* cool people did them. But she'd let it pass.

Maya studied the map to the Russell home then pulled out into traffic. "This one's in that new development off Snow Hill Road. We should be there in no time."

"This guy must be really cute, Bren," Morgan said, turning around in her seat. "But what if he has a girlfriend already?"

Bren blinked. She hadn't thought of that. He was new. He couldn't possibly have hooked up with somebody already—could he? "Well, then I may have to change that," she said airily.

Morgan laughed. She was only a year younger than Bren but was barely at the point where she noticed boys as anything more than possible friends. "Just don't be like Maya and try two dates in one night," she advised.

"If you ask me," Alex said to Bren, smirking, "that's one of the first things she's done right since I moved here."

Bren saw Maya's eyes narrowing in the rearview mirror. It was the first comment Alex had made since they dropped off Jamie.

"I'm with Maya totally," Alex continued. "I never want to get involved in a relationship." The word *relationship* came out as if it were synonymous with toxic waste.

Bren started to say something but decided against it. Of all the TodaysGirls, Alex seemed to struggle most. She constantly insisted that she had no interest in going to college, and she almost always took a cynical view of the world. Bren knew there was no sense in getting Alex worked up. Besides, they had just pulled onto Crocus Drive.

"What's the house number?" Maya asked.

Morgan picked up the paper Bren had given her sister. "Four sixty-two. The evens are on my side."

The small car eased up a street so new it was still dotted with cement mixers and builders' trucks. "There it is!" Morgan cried, pointing to a boxy white colonial with a Palladian window over the front door. "There's Lover Boy's brand-new house!"

Maya pulled into the cement drive, and Bren let out a scream. "What are you *doing*? What if he sees us?"

Maya shrugged. "Then we say, 'Nice house you got here,'" she laughed. "Don't worry, nobody's even home. It looks all closed up."

Bren craned her neck to get a good look at Christopher Russell's house. Now that she knew his name, she wanted to know everything about him. The house had a dark green front door with a wreath on it, but it didn't tell much about its owners, aside from the fact that they had enough cash to build a nice house.

"It's gorgeous, isn't it?" Bren asked. She imagined herself walking up the brick path to the green front door with Christopher's arm around her. No, that wouldn't be right. They'd glide into the garage and go in through the kitchen door more likely. It would be one of those big kitchens with an island and a huge table on one end—

"Oops!" Maya broke into the daydream. "Somebody's signaling to turn in here." She put Mr. Beep in reverse and prepared to back out of the drive.

Bren glanced over her shoulder. Panic bolted through her as she caught a glimpse of the dark green Jeep Cherokee waiting in the street. She let out an anguished yelp and ducked just as Maya pulled in front of it. They were almost back at the Gnosh before she dared to sit up and breathe again.

"Do you think he saw me?" she moaned.

"Of course not," Maya assured her.

"Sure he did," Alex said at the same time.

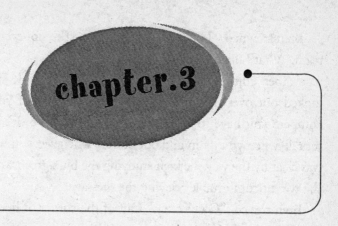

chapter.3

I can't believe the stuff that keeps happening!" Bren moaned at swim practice the next morning. "I'm not usually like this. You know I'm not like this. Right?"

"You need to chill," Maya replied. "You're getting obsessed with this guy." She stood at the edge of the pool working her arm and shoulder muscles to warm up.

"I guess so," Bren agreed. But her tone said she didn't really believe it. As far as she was concerned her friends were clueless when it came to true love.

"Good! You're here!" Amber called, emerging from Coach Short's office carrying his clipboard. She set it down on a deck chair and came over to join Bren and Maya. "You've got to start being more serious about practice, Bren."

Bren frowned. "I only missed twice. And I'm not even on the team. What's the big deal all of a sudden?"

Amber adjusted her red, white, and blue tank suit and looked out over the pool. "Coach says that even if you don't compete you have to be here on time every time. It's bad for morale when you fly in and out of here whenever you want." It was clear by the way she kept studying the blue-green water that she was uncomfortable relaying the message.

Bren sighed. "Okay, okay." Out of the corner of her eye she could see Coach Short coming out of his office.

"Bren!" he called. "Glad you could make it. We need you suited up and ready at every practice just like everyone else. Okay, girls, take your places. Time's a'wasting." He blew the silver whistle hanging from his thick neck and called out to a few stragglers still chatting by the doorway.

Bren shoved down her annoyance and took her place at the edge of the pool. Maya positioned herself in the lane to her right, and Amber claimed lane four to her left. Flexing her toes against the blue and white tiles of the decking, Bren thought about everything that had happened. Somehow she had to get to know Christopher Russell. Once he was her boyfriend, she knew they'd laugh at the previous crazy encounters.

At Coach Short's prompt, six girls hit the water almost simultaneously. Bren felt an adrenaline rush so strong it was almost electric. Her swimming skills were mediocre at best, but today she felt charged, like she could beat the record for swimming the English Channel. She kicked her feet furiously and lashed at the water with her arms. To her left she could see Amber inching ahead, but Maya was still behind her. Bren worked harder. Harder. *Harder*—as though all the stress over Christopher could be discharged through her muscles. She reached the side of the pool, tapped it, and reversed, this time not trying to gauge her position. She swam as though she were being chased by a school of sharks.

"Good job, Bren!" Coach Short congratulated her when she came in second following Amber. "Keep swimming like that and you may be competing after all. Your form could use some work, but you sure had the speed today."

Bren smiled at him. She knew exactly what he meant. Last month Maya's dad had made a video at practice. It showed her friends gliding like graceful dolphins, while she'd flailed at the water like a galumphing sheepdog.

Maya and Bren stood off to the side as six more girls lined up. Jamie walked by with a stack of clean towels. Her schedule at the Gnosh prevented her from being on the team, but she loved hanging out and helping at the pool.

"Hi guys," she greeted them. "How did it go yesterday? Did you identify Mystery Man?"

"Yup," Maya said. "He's one Christopher Russell. Still don't know him, but we did get a glimpse." She looked at Bren and smirked.

Bren groaned. "Oh, Jamie, it was awful! I tried to call you last night, but your phone was tied up forever. I sent you an e-mail for whenever you got off the line. Who were you talking to?"

Jamie's brow puckered. "Mom was talking to that Jack guy again. I think he's advising her about a career move." She grinned. *"Career*—got that? Not romance. I never did check my in-box. I got home late, and Jessica was still awake, all in a panic because she had to draw a map. By the time I finished helping her, I barely had time to write my essay for English."

"It was awful!" Bren repeated. "He came home while we were parked in his driveway! I think he saw me."

Jamie shifted the towels to her other arm. "Why am I not surprised?" she asked with obvious amusement. "I don't have a clue who this Christopher is, but whoever he is, I sure hope he's worth it. Listen, we'll talk later. I gotta get these in the locker room and dash. I need to proof my essay."

When Jamie was gone, Maya let out a long sigh. "I shouldn't tease you," she told Bren. "I'm not exactly winning the dating game myself these days."

Bren raised her eyebrows. "But I thought . . ."

Coach Short blew his whistle. "This is not a gabfest, girls!" he hollered. "Let's get with it here! Maya! Bren! To your marks!"

Bren had to wait until the team was crowded into the steamy locker room to find out what Maya was talking about.

"What happened to the two dates for Saturday night?" Bren asked after they emerged from the showers.

"Seems I made a tactical error," Maya answered, gently patting her face dry with a towel. "Date A turned out to be Date B's *cousin*. Who knew?" She tossed the wet towel into a nearby hamper. "The bottom line is I'm now dateless, and they're both mad at me."

Amber pulled a pair of jeans from her bag and sighed. "Dateless. That's the story of my entire life. Would you believe I haven't been asked out once this entire year?"

"Me either," Morgan said cheerfully.

Amber smiled at Maya's younger sister. "You just wait," she said kindly. "The time's coming when you'll have so many dates you won't know how—or who—to choose."

Morgan grinned. "Well, it better not be too soon, because I don't think Dad will let me anywhere near a car with a boy until I'm sixteen. That's almost two years."

Bren remembered when she hadn't dated yet either. Life had been so much easier then. The biggest thing on her mind had been which movie to rent or game to play. In some ways, she wished she could turn back the clock. Love was hard. But of course if it worked out—and it *had* to work out—it was wonderful. The thought cheered her up. She reached into her gym bag and pulled out her favorite brush.

"You guys are nuts with this dating thing," Alex offered, wriggling her fingers through a few strands of her soaking-wet mahogany hair. "The only way I'd go out with a guy is if he had courtside seats at a Pacers game."

Bren started to say something about the merits of a good herbal conditioner, but she decided against it. Alex didn't like beauty tips any better than she liked dating.

"A Pacers game! Girl, do you have any idea what kind of cash you're talking for courtside tickets?" Maya demanded. "You keep making up requirements like that, and you won't date anyone ever. At least not in high school."

Alex shrugged. "When I have a job, I'll get my own tickets then. You have to get what you want your own way. And Bren, if you wanna go out with dude, you might check how low you rank on the assertiveness chart."

Bren plugged in her hair dryer, glad for once that the deafening roar prevented her from talking. She thought about Alex's last remark while she lifted handfuls of hair. Maybe there was a germ of truth in it—at least in the part about being more assertive. Maybe it was time to stop waiting for Christopher Russell to notice her. She should let him know she'd noticed *him.* She switched off the dryer and turned to her friends.

"I've just made a decision," she announced, brandishing the salon-quality dryer. "I am no longer waiting for Mr. Russell to get his act together. I'm going to march down the hall before last block and seize him at the gym doors."

Maya burst out laughing. "You're going to *what?*"

Bren giggled. "Well, okay, not exactly seize him, but seize the moment. You know—*carpe diem*—seize the day? It's Latin. I'll ask him for a date myself. What do you guys think?"

"You go, girl!" Maya laughed. "Just let me go with you. I wouldn't miss this if the entire stock of my new dELiA*s catalog was being delivered to my doorstep."

Bren put down the dryer. She felt less confident, now that she'd made her announcement. Like someone who's just made a promise that she's not really sure she can keep.

"What should I say?" she asked. "I've never asked a guy out in my entire life. Well, maybe I sort of hinted once. You know—that time we were at the pool last summer and that cousin of Brad Moore's was here visiting from Kentucky, and I sort of mentioned the county fair and how much I love the lights on the midway at night? Oh, it's sooooo magical! And don't even get me started about the Ferris wheel when it's lit up!" Bren rolled her eyes and pretended to swoon.

Maya snapped her fingers in front of Bren's face. "Focus!" she demanded. "Focus! Christopher Russell. Date. Game plan."

Bren's attention popped back to the locker room. "Yes, game plan. Uh—I don't have one," she admitted.

Morgan popped her head through the neck hole of her T-shirt. "How about this, Bren? Get dressed, open the door, walk through it, go find Christopher Russell, and ask him to go to a movie."

"But I don't even know where he is first block, and what if he says no?" Bren wailed. "I'd die. I'd just lay down and die."

"You would not die," Maya said firmly. "You'd be disappointed.

Hurt. Crushed. Devastated. Humiliated. Sad even. But you would not die."

"And don't worry about where he is, Ms. Seize of the Day," added the ever-positive Morgan. "Just ask him when you see him."

Bren sighed. Love was so much more complicated than her friends could ever imagine. It was like her heart had spread itself across a battlefield with a battalion in combat boots stomping across it. They were right about one thing though. It was definitely time to take action. She would do it! *As soon as I see him again*, she thought, *I'll do it. Before I lose my nerve.*

"You're right, Morgan. Give me five minutes, and we're outta here," she said with new resolve.

She pulled on a short gray pleated skirt, an orange baby-tee, and a gray velour jacket. She zipped the jacket precisely halfway up, pulled on a pair of short gray patterned socks, and topped them off with gray suede hiking boots. A touch of mascara, a skim of peach blush, a slick of tangerine gloss, and she was ready and on her way to seize.

"I wish Jamie could see this," said Maya, scurrying to keep up with Bren. "She'll be sorry she missed it."

"Where is she, anyway?" asked Amber from behind.

"Proofing her English paper," Bren answered over her shoulder.

"Well, I'm worried about her," Amber sais as they merged into the wider main hall to walk side by side. "She said her mom's acting wierd, and I'm praying it's not money problems. College is right around the corner, and both Jamie and Ms. Chandler are working as hard as they can. I hope it's nothing."

"Are you serious?" Maya asked. "She hasn't said anything to me about it."

Bren didn't comment. She doubted there was a problem—or at least not the kind Jamie suspected. *How could they be so dense?* Bren wondered. She began scanning faces for one in particular, listening to her girlfriends prattle.

"Anyway, we need to be supportive," Amber continued. "I'm putting her on my personal prayer list. I'd put her on the chain at church, but she'd be embarrassed."

"True," Maya agreed. "I'll see if I can talk to her tonight. Maybe I can give her a ride to the Gnosh." The girls turned the corner by the media center, surveying the hall for Christopher Russell.

"I don't see him anywhere," said Morgan.

"Me either," added Amber, glancing at her watch. "I'm sorry," she said, "but I can't be late for this class again. Mr. Kistler said he'd make me stay after if it ever happened again."

"No problem," Bren responded, tearing her eyes away from her search. "It's okay—really."

"We're outta here, too," added Alex, heading toward study hall, pulling Morgan along by the edge of a sleeve.

"This is serious, Bren," Maya said as soon as the two were alone. "Will you try to talk to Jamie? You're closer to her than anybody."

"Yeah, I'll talk to her," Bren agreed, focusing on Maya's sincere anxiety about their friend. "But the truth is, there is absolutely nothing to . . ."

"Look! There she is now!" Maya cried. "Jamie! Hey!"

Bren looked where Maya was waving. She froze. Jamie stood at the end of the hall, laughing with Christopher Russell, his arm encircling her shoulders!

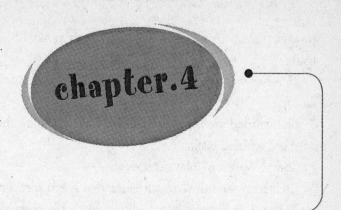

chapter.4

I don't have a clue who this Christopher is . . .

Jamie's words pounded in Bren's brain. Beside her, Bren could hear Maya's sharp intake of breath. Maya put her hand firmly on Bren's arm. Jerking away, Bren stalked toward Jamie and Christopher.

"How *could* you?" she screamed at Jamie. "How could you stand there and lie to me like that? Did you think I wouldn't find out? How dumb do you think I am?"

Jamie's eyes widened with confusion. "I don't . . ."

"Oh, please—save the innocent act! I know what you're up to. I just can't believe you'd do something like this to me!" Bren knew she was creating a scene, but now that her feelings had come tumbling out, there was no stopping them.

"Bren," Maya said quietly. She placed her hand on Bren's

arm, as though to pull her away, but Bren yanked herself free again.

"I never want to speak to you again, Jamie Chandler!" she shouted.

She whirled around, remembered she was going the wrong way, and whirled back.

"Bren! Wait up!" Maya called.

Bren barely heard Maya tell Jamie that they'd sort it out later. Well, they *wouldn't* sort it out, she decided. Her friendship with Jamie Chandler was over. She ducked into first block, leaving Maya in the hall. Everybody would probably take Jamie's side. Jamie was always so perfect, so reasonable, so sensible. What they didn't know, and probably wouldn't believe, was that it was all an act.

Jamie Chandler is a big, fat liar, Bren thought bitterly, *and all this time, she was just pretending to be my best friend.* Bren fought back angry tears for the rest of the morning.

Later, in the cafeteria, Bren didn't know what to do. Maya, Amber, and Jamie were already at their usual table when she came in for lunch. She wouldn't have lunch today, she decided. She wasn't hungry anyway. She turned to leave just as Jamie hurried over.

"Wait! Bren!"

Bren hesitated. She didn't want to hear Jamie's excuses. But on the other hand, she had to find out whether or not Jamie and Christopher were really an item.

"Please, Bren! Can I talk to you? Can we go somewhere?" Jamie asked.

Bren shrugged.

"Come on. Let's go sit in the Commons. We need to talk." Jamie led the way to the large area at the front of the school where everybody hung out during free time. At this hour, it was practically deserted.

Jamie pulled her ball cap out of her pocket and sat down on the top step leading to the sunken area by the front doors. Bren sat down beside her. "This better be good," Bren warned.

Jamie put on her cap and took a deep breath. "Bren," she started, "I honestly don't know what you're mad about. I really don't."

Bren jumped to her feet, fury racing through her veins again. "How can you sit there and say that to me?" she demanded. "You know how I feel about Christopher! And there you were, all over him, right under my nose! In front of everyone! You—"

Bren stopped in mid-shout. The look on Jamie's face was so genuinely confused and sorrowful.

"Who is Christopher?" Jamie asked in the momentary silence.

"The blond with his arm around you. *My* Christopher," Bren said. It was her turn to be confused. Either Jamie should win an Oscar, or she really didn't know Christopher's name.

Jamie slapped both hands to the sides of her face and let out a groan. "You mean Russ? *Russ* is your mystery man?"

"Who is Russ?"

"The guy I was with. His name is Russ. That's what the teachers call him. He's in my calculus class. He was born in Chicago and I was wearing my White Sox cap, so he asked me if I was a fan. He got all chummy—he said my hat made him feel like he was back home. It's no big deal. He's not interested in me, and I'm not interested in him. We barely know each other."

Bren looked into Jamie's eyes and knew her friend was telling the truth. "Oh, Jamie, I feel so awful for thinking you'd hurt me like that!" she wailed. She plopped back down on the step and clasped her knees. Her toes pointed at each other like two accusing fingers. "I am sooooo stupid."

Jamie sat beside her. "I can see how it happened," she said quietly. "But Bren, I wouldn't do something like that. I wouldn't."

Bren reached over and gave Jamie a hug. "I know that. I really do. It's just this whole being in love thing. It's got my brain so messed up that . . . "

Jamie started to say something but stopped.

"Do you forgive me?" Bren asked.

"Of course I do." Jamie started to get up, but Bren pulled her back down.

"What's this thing with your mom?" she asked. "Everybody's worried about you. I guess I've been so wrapped up in my own problems, I haven't been paying attention. I'm sorry."

Jamie sighed. "I don't know, Bren. She's still talking to this

Jack guy all the time. I'd never heard of him before, and now he's on the phone every night. She told me they've had coffee together several times, and she's met him for dinner twice. But I know they're not hooking up. It's about business."

"So why are you so worried then?" Bren asked. "If he helps her get a better job, it can only be good, right?"

Jamie shook her head. "I don't think so," she said slowly. "She loves her job. She'd never leave it unless there was something wrong. Either she's getting laid off, or she needs more money. I thought I heard her say something about the roof— like the cost is through the roof, or the roof over our heads. Something. What if we have to move? I'm freaking out."

Bren didn't reply for several seconds. She had no idea what it meant to worry about money. Her dad was a doctor who could afford to give his family every privilege. Poor Jamie had to struggle for everything she got.

"Amber said she'd say special prayers for you," she said finally. "And I'll help in any way I can. Just find out what's going on and tell me what you need."

Jamie stood up. "Thanks, Bren. You're the best."

The girls headed back to the lunchroom, their mood lifting as they imagined what the rest of their friends must be thinking about their fight.

"I can already hear the wheels turning in Amber's head," Jamie chortled. "She'll write a Thought for the Day about friendship and have it posted before we log on tonight."

"Yeah, she will, while Maya writes her speech about group loyalty. And Morgan will be wringing her hands in between self-help Web sites for relationship counseling," Bren agreed.

"And Alex will be e-mailing everyone in town that we're both total nuts," Jamie continued. "And then she'll tell us that her friends were sane back in Texas . . ."

Bren suddenly let out a strangled yelp and ducked into the rest room, leaving Jamie chattering to herself. Christopher Russell—*Russ*—had just rounded the corner! She leaned against the wall and closed her eyes. No way could she ask him for a date *now*. Love kept getting harder and harder. When would the good part start?

Fifteen minutes later, Bren slipped into her desk next to Jamie's in English. Until now, Bren hadn't been able to wait to read her poem, but now she felt like she'd just finished running the Boston Marathon. Mr. J.W. Bailey obviously didn't realize her dilemma, though, because he called on her first.

Bren smoothed out the pleats in her skirt and went to the front of the room. Her poem was called "The River." The whole thing was incredibly romantic, but the part she'd remembered from her first reading in her dad's office was the best: "My pent-up tears oppress my brain, my heart is swollen with love unsaid. Oh, let me weep and tell my pain, and onto thy shoulder rest my head." Even though she read those lines with extra feeling, her reading did little to ease her own emotional exhaustion.

"Very good, Bren," Mr. Bailey said when she finished. "Now

tell us why you chose that particular poem. It's a bit obscure. Arnold is most noted for *Dover Beach*."

Bren tucked one side of her hair behind her ear. Now that she was standing in front of thirty-three people talking about love, she felt less sure of herself. The good news was that Christopher—*Russ*—wasn't in the class.

"I chose this poem because it speaks so deeply about the pain of falling in love," she said. "The poet is clearly writing from his heart. You can tell this if you've ever written anything from your own heart. It's like me when I keep my journal. Of course I don't keep it very well. I *mean* to, but I get busy. There was this one time, though, that I did it for three whole weeks and then—"

Mr. Bailey offered his ghost of a smile. "Thank you, Bren," he interrupted softly. "We get the picture."

Jamie was next. She walked up to the front of the room carrying a sheet of neatly typed paper.

"Mine isn't exactly a poem," she explained. "But you said we could choose anything. This is an excerpt from the Bible, and I chose it after my mom told me that this passage is the truest thing she ever read about love. I don't always agree with my mom, but she's right on this one, because love is about a lot more than just romance."

Jamie must have looked up the entire text in the Bible, because what she read was longer than the quote on the bookmark. "'. . . So these three things continue forever: faith, hope and love. And the greatest of these is love,'" she ended.

In the back of the room, Mr. Bailey was silent for a moment. "You have a very wise mother, Miss Chandler," he said quietly. "Martin, would you like to be next?"

Geeky Martin Johnson from the yearbook staff took Jamie's place. Bren knew he'd done her a favor by getting the student list to Jamie, but Bren tuned him out anyway. Why had she babbled on about her journal? Mr. Bailey clearly thought Jamie's selection was better than hers. She knew she hadn't managed what she'd *meant* to say about the pain of love. She sighed. All she wanted to do was go home and sign into the chat room. If there ever had been a time when she needed her friends, this was definitely it.

After class, she and Jamie headed out the door.

"That was some poem you read," Jamie said with a giggle. "Onto thy shoulder rest my head?"

Bren shrugged. "It's romantic, okay?"

"If you say so." Jamie shrugged back.

"No, seriously, Jamie. Think about how comforting that would be, like in the throes of pain and heartache, you could just lay your head on his shoulder, and then—"

"Hey Bren!" Martin called.

Bren stopped and turned around, surprised. She'd never spoken to Martin Johnson in her life, and he'd never spoken to her. Surely Jamie hadn't told him *why* she needed that list.

He adjusted his glasses and smiled. "Two things," he said. "First of all, great outfit. The boots are an unusual choice, but

42

they work. It's the length of the skirt and the pleats I think. Good proportion."

Bren blinked. He was absolutely right! How in the world did Martin Johnson know anything about fashion design? Most of the time, he looked like an unmade bed.

"Th-thanks," she mumbled.

Martin grinned. "Second thing. I'm curious about your poetry selection. Do you really believe that love is so . . ."—he stammered, groping for a word—"so anguished?"

Bren sighed. *Here we go again,* she thought. Another person who doesn't know what it means to be so totally in love you can barely think, much less breathe and talk and do the million other things you have to do in a day. "Of course I do," she said. "And if you'd ever been in love you'd know that."

She started to turn away, but Martin stopped her. "I've never been in love," he said slowly. "But I don't think real love is about suffering. That seems like such an ego trip to me—no offense," he added. "If you love somebody, you're just happy they're around, happy when they're happy. I'm probably not making any sense." He stopped as a deep crimson blush crawled noticeably up his neck.

"No, I think you're right, Martin," Jamie said. "It's like it said in my selection, 'And the greatest of these is love.' Love is a human being reaching his or her highest aspirations."

Martin's face lit up. "Yes!" he cried. "Like Mother Teresa, for example . . ."

Bren rolled her eyes. "I'll catch up with you later, Jamie. Remember to log on at five."

She walked down the hall alone. Martin Johnson was the weirdest guy on the planet. Why Jamie spent time yakking to him about love was beyond her. But in a way she was glad he'd intruded because she could use some time alone to decide what to do next. Asking Russ out was no longer an option. She wasn't ready to face him, much less set herself up for some rejection. Somehow she had to find a way to get together with him that seemed more—accidental.

At home, Bren raced up the curving staircase to her room. If only she could think of some great ruse to "accidentally" throw her and Russ together. She knew she could count on her friends to help pull it off. Someone would have an idea. She turned the corner and nearly crashed headlong into her mother.

"Bren!" Mrs. Mickler said, laughing. "You nearly mowed me down. Where's the fire?"

Bren laughed. "Sorry. No fire. Just a hard day." She walked down the hall to her room, hoping her mother would get the point that she wanted to be alone.

She didn't.

"Anything I can do to help?" Mrs. Mickler asked as Bren dropped her bags on the floor and collapsed onto her bed.

"Looks like boy trouble to me," she pressed when Bren didn't say anything. Mrs. Mickler sat down on the edge of the bed and waited.

Bren considered changing the subject but decided to ask anyway. "Mom, did you ever want to meet a guy but not want to be like obvious?" she asked. She made her voice sound light, as though it were no big deal.

Mrs. Mickler flipped her thick black hair over her shoulder and giggled. It was a young girl's gesture, one that surprised Bren. Her mother was beautiful—with her deep dancing eyes, flawless Filipino skin, and that wide Julia Roberts smile. But Bren found it hard to believe her mom had ever been fifteen and a half.

"Sure," she said. "What girl hasn't? I remember the first time I came to the United States during my last year of school."

"When you were a foreign exchange student?" Bren supplied.

Mrs. Mickler nodded and lay back next to her daughter on the bed.

"Yeah, I was staying with a family in Atlanta, and there was a boy at school that I was just crazy about. Now this was back when computers were huge monsters—very expensive—and of course nobody but universities and the government even had them."

"Sooooo?" Bren hated to hurry the story, but she was uninterested in a lecture on the history of computer science.

Mrs. Mickler chuckled at the impatience. "The school must have had access to one through some agency or college, because we held a dance, and all the dates were matched by that computer. It was hilarious, really, because the guy I was so crazy about—"

Bren bolted upright and leaped over her mother's body to the floor. "That's it! That's it!" she screeched, jumping and waving like she was in the middle of a halftime performance. "Thank you, Mommy! Thank you, thank you, thank you!"

Mrs. Mickler sat up. "Glad to help," she said, smiling. Bren hardly noticed her mother leaving the room as she started searching the Web.

At precisely 5:00 P.M., Bren logged on to the TodaysGirls.com Web site and tapped in her password. She was so excited that it took three tries to get it right. As soon as she was allowed access, Bren clicked past Amber's "thought" again and went straight into the chat room. She could see the list of users, but she typed anyway:

chicChick: Anybody in here?

Maya and Amber responded immediately.

nycbutterfly: half of us. U feeling better?
faithful1: I'm here. Worried about u

Bren smiled to herself. She was glad they weren't mad at her for biting Jamie's head off.

chicChick: I need ur help. Got an idea!
jellybean: Hold on a minute. Maya, Mom just said u have
    2 pick up Dad.

faithful1: What's ur idea?
chicChick: Computer dating.
nycbutterfly: How retro!
jellybean: What's computer dating?
faithful1: 2 kewl!
jellybean: What's computer dating?
chicChick: nu u'd luv it!
jellybean: WHAT'S COMPUTER DATING?

chapter.5

The next day, everyone met at Bren's house after school. Her upstairs suite, with its own private bath and living area—was ideal for mapping out their plans to launch the dating service. Maya had explained computer dating to Morgan, who in turn had explained it to Alex, so everybody understood that the idea was to feed the computer information about the people seeking dates, and the machine would make the matches based on compatible answers to a questionnaire.

"Okay, the first thing we need to do is figure out how to market the idea," Maya said, her eyes panning her friends' faces encircling Bren's oversized coffee table.

"We have the database Martin gave me when we were looking for Mr. Wonderful," Jamie said, flashing Bren a quick grin.

"It lists e-mail addresses for everybody in the whole school who has one. We could send a mass e-mail."

"Spam City!" Alex crowed. She grabbed a pillow from the couch, bunched it up behind her head, and stretched out on the floor.

Amber shrugged. "Call it whatever you want, but I need this to work. Remember, I'm the one who's been dateless all year!"

"But what about reaching all the people who don't have a computer or Internet access?" Morgan asked, flopping back on the couch. "Just imagine . . . life without the Internet. Just like in the olden days," she mused wonderingly.

The room went quiet as everyone thought about a way to reach the cyber-impaired.

"We'll make a flyer," Jamie said finally, grabbing a pen from her bag. "They won't let us post it at school. Only clubs and school-sanctioned stuff can go up. Oh, I know! The Gnosh! Do you think your dad would let us hang a flyer on his board? And maybe put a stack of questionnaires on the counter?" she asked Maya and Morgan.

"He'll do it," Maya said quickly. "I'll talk to him. That's perfect. *Everybody* comes to the Gnosh sooner or later."

"Okay, but I still don't see how the computer is going to match anybody up," Morgan cut in. "Let's get to that part."

"Yup, that's definitely the most complicated aspect," Amber agreed. "But not to worry. I know how to do it." She took a sheet of notebook paper from her three-ring binder. "First, we make up a list of questions. Once we've gotten them back completed, we'll need to create a record for each individual. The collection of records forms the database. I've already found a free program on the Web and downloaded it to my computer."

"Rock!" Jamie cried. "So you found one that'll let us create a query?" she continued, pulling some loose-leaf paper from Amber's binder to start their to-do list.

"A what?" asked Morgan.

"Good question," Amber said. "We just learned about them last night. That means we can tell the computer which answers absolutely must be identical before a match is made and which ones must *not* match. It will also allow us to program the number of positive matches required to pair two people up. We may have to fool around with it a little to determine how many positives we want."

"This is so cool!" Bren squealed. "Isn't this cool?"

"I'm underwhelmed," Alex said.

Jamie tapped her pen impatiently. "What kind of questions do we want besides the usual name, address, e-mail address, phone number, age, gender, and year in school?"

"Career goals," Amber said. "I'd love to go out with somebody who wants to be a writer too. Oh, yeah, and let's add GPA. I don't want somebody dumber than me." She giggled. "Wait! That didn't come out right. What I meant to say is I don't want someone who isn't as dedicated to school as I am."

Maya cocked an elegant eyebrow at her friend. "Sure, Amber. That's just what you meant."

"We ought to have favorites, too," Morgan piped up, idly perusing Bren's stack of new CDs on the end table. "Like music, sports, movies, food, school organizations, stuff like that."

"And I want to see some personality questions," Maya added.

Bren slid down the edge of the couch to sit cross-legged on the floor. "Oh, me, too!" she agreed. "Like, 'Would you call yourself the *romantic* type?'"

Alex pulled the pillow from behind her head and tossed it at Bren. "Oh yeah, like guys would admit that on paper," she cried.

Bren clasped the pillow to her chest. "'How do I love thee?'" she intoned. "'Let my computer count the ways!'" She fell over in a crumpled heap and burst into giggles.

"Looks like the old Bren is back," Jamie said, nudging Bren with her toe.

Bren sat up, a little surprised at her own silliness. It seemed like ages since she'd been able to just hang with her friends. Ever since she'd fallen in love, life had become decidedly unfunny.

They worked for another half-hour developing potential questions. When they were finished, they had thirty.

"Perfect," Bren said, looking over Jamie's shoulder. "Just enough to make it interesting, but not so many that people will get bored."

"I've got to get to work," Jamie answered, "but I'll get it typed up and make copies at the library tomorrow. Maya, you ask your dad about putting the questionnaires at the Gnosh.

Bren, you get online with Amber tonight, and get that program loaded over here where we've got more megs. Morgan, you write up the e-mail message . . ."

"Spam," Alex corrected.

"And I'll send it to everybody on Martin's database," Bren interrupted. "And Alex, you can help Morgan write the 'spam.' The two of you can also talk it up with the freshmen."

Jamie stood up and headed for the door. "A ride would be nice," she hinted at Maya.

Maya grinned and stood up too. "You got it. Come on, guys," she said to the younger girls. "Mr. Beep awaits."

A week later, the plans were in place. Mr. Cross had agreed to advertise the dating service at the Gnosh, the e-mail had been sent to everyone in the student body who had an e-mail address, and a stack of questionnaires waited to be distributed. The first day they were available, Bren stood waiting at Jamie's locker when she arrived at school.

"I need your help," Bren said as Jamie came up to her. "You've got to make sure Russ signs up, okay?"

"Sure," Jamie replied. "No problem." She balanced her books in one arm and twirled the dial on her combination lock with the opposite hand. "But what if you two don't match up? It could happen, you know."

Bren tucked her hair behind her ear. "It won't," she said confidently. "We're meant to be together. I *know* it. I can *feel* it."

Jamie frowned as she opened her locker door. "Well, maybe. I hope you're right. But I'd hate to see you get your hopes up and end up disappointed, Bren. We don't even know him."

"Just get him to fill out the form," Bren said with a touch of annoyance. "The rest will take care of itself. Do it this morning, okay?"

"Okay," Jamie agreed.

By lunchtime, Bren felt like a flock of luna moths was dancing the *Nutcracker Suite* in her stomach. She raced to the cafeteria and flung herself into the chair next to Jamie's.

"Well?" she demanded.

Jamie carefully unwrapped her peanut butter and jelly sandwich. "He doesn't have a computer."

"Whaaaaaaaat?" Bren screeched. "Get outta town. We saw his house. There's gotta be a computer in there."

Jamie nodded. "It's his dad. He won't allow a computer in the house—with or without the Web. AND he thinks the government tracks Internet users to find out everything about their lives."

Bren stared at her open-mouthed. "Huh? That is the craziest thing I ever heard. How could they do that?"

Jamie took a bite of sandwich and chewed thoughtfully. "I think it's a little paranoid too," she agreed. "But actually companies track Net users all the time—so they can sell us stuff."

"Marketing, I know," Bren said. "But the government?"

"All I know," Jamie answered, "is that Amber said that every time you visit a site, your computer makes something called a 'cookie,' which lets anyone who wants to bother checking know exactly where you've been. It stays a permanent part of your Internet profile even if you buy a new machine. Really, anybody could find out what you do online. I don't get to spend enough time online to think about it, but—"

"Okay, so he doesn't have a computer," Bren interrupted. "Does that mean he can't fill out a form? He can't be illiterate."

Jamie shook her head. "No, but I'm not sure he really wants to participate. He doesn't seem to trust computers any more than his dad does."

"That's ridiculous! WORK ON HIM!" Bren yelled. Several people at surrounding tables turned to look at her, but she ignored them. "We have to get his answers into the computer, or my idea is dead. Why do you think I even thought this whole thing up in the first place?"

"Okay, okay—no stress. I'll try again later today," Jamie promised.

Bren went to English with her stomach tied in knots. If Russ didn't complete a questionnaire, she might as well not even have suggested the computer dating service. What was the point? There was no one else she wanted to be matched up with.

"Hey, Bren!" Martin Johnson called as she slid into her seat. "I filled out one of your forms for the computer dating service and e-mailed it to you."

Bren smiled weakly. "That's good," she murmured.

Martin came over and leaned against Jamie's empty desk. "Yeah, I think it's a cool idea, computer dating," he offered. "It sort of cuts to the chase. At least you know going in you have something in common with the person. But then again, it can only be as good as its programmer."

"It'll be fine," Bren replied. "Amber knows a lot about computers, and I'm sure she'll do it right." She opened her book and made a show of being wildly interested in page twenty-three.

Martin adjusted his glasses. "By the way, nice ensemble again. You really have an innate sense of style."

Bren had picked out what she was wearing with the same judicious care she'd given to choosing school clothes every single day since she'd first spotted Christopher Russell. The short green plaid kilt, white turtleneck, and killer knee-high socks in a matching plaid looked sensational with her chunky-heeled black platform shoes. Supermodel Rabeka Roundtree had worn the exact same outfit in a back issue of *Modena* magazine.

"Thanks. But I can't take credit for this one. Bought it right off the rack, as modeled. How come you're so interested in clothes?" she asked.

The tips of Martin's ears reddened. He shifted uncomfortably and looked down at the tiled floor. "I don't know. I might be interested in doing some designing some day," he muttered.

Bren couldn't believe her ears. Martin looked about as much like a designer as she looked like a pro wrestler. She mumbled something about that being cool and breathed a sigh of relief when J.W. Bailey strode into the room and called for order.

Jamie flopped, breathless, into the desk beside her just as the bell rang. "Here," she whispered. "I was almost late because of you." She handed Bren a completed form for the dating service.

Bren saw the name at the top—Christopher Russell—and suppressed a squeal. She whispered a quick "thank-you" and stuck the form in her notebook. The last thing she wanted to risk was its being confiscated by the substitute. Everyone else still had to read their love poems, and Mr. Bailey would expect her to pay attention. But as the voices droned on, Bren couldn't resist a few quick peeks at Russ's form. He loved pizza. So did she! He considered himself romantic. Her heart did a backflip. He loved adventure movies. Well, she could tolerate them—no problem there. He liked animals and had a dog. That was good. A guy who liked animals had to be warm and fuzzy. She smiled and closed the notebook.

The Cleopatra girl's best friend was just beginning a long, awkward rendition of "How Do I Love Thee?" Bren sighed and decided to take one last peek. He liked watching baseball. Well, that was a typical enough guy thing, but what had he written underneath it? Bren took out her glasses and perched them on her nose to decipher the handwriting. A thought had popped into her head when she read it the first time, but it was too funny to be right. She read it again, closed the notebook, and took off her glasses. There was no mistake. Christopher Russell, the man of her dreams, liked—*bowling!* In fact, he liked bowling so much he'd underlined it twice!

Bren tried to catch Jamie's eye, but she was listening intently to the butchering of "How Do I Love Thee?" What was she going to do now? She'd never been in a bowling alley in her entire life. Nobody she knew bowled except Amber and Morgan. Was it possible to not like bowling and still be matched with him? She couldn't remember how many questions, or even which questions, they'd decided had to match.

"Psssst! Jamie!" She kept an eye on Mr. Bailey as she tried to get Jamie's attention.

Jamie looked over and raised her eyebrows.

"He likes bowling!" she whispered. *"Bowling!"*

Mr. Bailey was standing at the side of the room, gazing out the window as he listened to the laborious reading of a poem he could probably recite in his sleep. He looked over at Bren.

"Excuse me, Miss Arthur." He held up his hand to halt the girl at the front of the class. "I believe Miss Mickler has something extremely important she'd like to tell us about bowling."

The class cracked up.

Bren thought quickly. "What I meant to say," she said smoothly, "is that those *Sonnets from the Portuguese* are forever bowling me over. Every time I hear 'How Do I Love Thee?' I'm just . . . well, bowled over."

The class laughed again. Someone in the back of the room

applauded. Bren turned her head just enough to see that it was Martin.

Mr. Bailey did that ghost smile thing again. "Good one, Miss Mickler," he said. "An excellent save."

After class, Bren grabbed Jamie's arm and dragged her into the hall before Martin could corner them again. "What am I going to do?" Bren demanded. "Do I need to take a crash course in bowling?"

Jamie laughed. "Of course not! Not every single question has to match, especially on the likes and dislikes questions. We ended up putting more importance on values, remember?"

Bren heaved a sigh of relief. "That's right! You're right. I'm losing it."

Jamie nodded. "You are, Bren," she said seriously. "You've been losing it ever since you got this crush on him. You don't even know him yet. And I really don't want you to get hurt."

"I won't," Bren snapped. She hadn't meant to sound so abrupt. But the tone had crept into Bren's voice as if it had a will of its own. "Sorry," she said quickly. "It's just that I feel so sure we're going to match up. I don't want one thing to ruin it."

At home, Bren went straight to her computer. Amber had loaded their dating program on Bren's computer, since it had the most memory and speed. And since Bren had the program, Jamie had entered Bren's e-mail address for returning all questionnaires.

Bren switched on her PC and logged on to the Internet. Her eyes popped when she hit her mail icon. Eighty-seven messages! Last night, there had been twenty-two within two hours of Jamie's sending the mass e-mail. Most of the respondents had filled out their information online. Bren printed out a third of the messages and put them into a folder. It was going to take hours to create this many records. She might as well get started.

She pulled Russ's form from her notebook, opened the dating program, and began entering his information. By the time she had reached the twentieth form, she was grateful Amber had used a program that provided for "sticky fields." That way all she had to do was type "bas" and "basketball" immediately appeared in the sports field, or "pi" and "pizza" popped up under favorite food. She worked so long that she missed the regular 5:00 P.M. meeting in the chat room. When she finally remembered to log on, no one was there.

Mrs. Mickler tapped on the partly open door. "Bren? It's time for dinner."

Bren saved her work and turned off just her monitor. She would try to get back to it after dinner, she decided as she bounded down the steps. *Yeah*, she reminded herself, *and after the rest of my homework, too.* She slid in her sock feet across the dining room floor and into the kitchen, where her dad was setting the table.

"Hi, honey," he called.."How's ComputerDating.com?"

"It's TodaysGirls.com, Daddy," she corrected him. "The

computer dating is just something we're doing. You know it was all Mom's idea."

"She never needed any computers to get a date with me," he smiled, openly admiring his wife as he pulled Bren's chair out from the table for her. Mrs. Mickler stood at the island cooktop, flashing Dr. Mickler a wide smile as she ladled steaming *adobo* onto a bed of white rice.

Filling the room with its fragrant combination aroma of chicken, pork, soy sauce, and garlic, her mom's famous *adobo* reminded Bren that she hadn't eaten since lunch.

"Don't you look at me like that," Mrs. Mickler teased her husband, waving her spoon at him as she deposited the large platter on the kitchen table.

Bren listened to her parents' easy banter with interest. She'd never really paid much attention to their relationship before now. They got along well, and that had been good enough for her. But now that she was in love herself, it was different.

She knew her parents had met in the Philippines when her father was volunteering with Doctors Without Borders, an organization that sends physicians all over the world to give free medical care to underdeveloped areas. Her dad had been work-ing with the street children of Manila and had taken a mini-break to go snorkeling with a friend when he'd met her beautiful mother on the beach.

"Did you guys fall in love at first sight?" she asked them now, carefully unfolding her napkin. She didn't want to sound *too* interested, or her mother would know there was a reason for this sudden curiosity. She wasn't ready to talk to them about Russ— not just yet.

"Oh, yeah!" her father said immediately.

"No way!" her mother said at the exact same moment.

Bren laughed. "So which one was it?"

"Both, really," Dr. Mickler explained. "We *were* immediately attracted to one another. What your *mother* means is that love came after we became the best of friends. Right, Cita?"

"Right," Mrs. Mickler agreed.

Bren didn't say anything. There were probably as many ways of falling in love as there were couples, she thought. *But for me and Russ,* she decided, *love will wash over us like a tidal wave.*

chapter.6

Maya handed Bren a stack of completed questionnaires that she'd been collecting at school all week. "Here's another thirty," Maya said. "You're lucky most people e-mailed theirs."

All of the TodaysGirls were back in Bren's suite, working their way through the huge pile of e-mailed questionnaires that Bren had printed off her computer.

"We're up to three hundred and forty-seven," Morgan announced, "plus whatever Maya has there."

"I've got some too," Alex said.

Every head in the room turned to look at her. Nobody had expected Alex to offer up anything more than wry comments.

"Good grief," she muttered. "No reason to freak. I've only

got sixteen." She rooted around in her army surplus knapsack and handed over a sheaf of crumpled pages.

"Is yours in here?" Bren asked her.

Alex shrugged. "Yeah, but only because you wouldn't get off my case if I didn't do it," she mumbled.

"Oh nooooo!" Bren moaned as she took the papers. "I just thought of something terrible! What if most of these forms are from girls? I noticed an awful lot of girls' names when I was keying them in."

Jamie covered her face with both hands and groaned. "I never thought of that! If that's the case, we've got a big problem. We better start sorting before we do anything else. I've gotta get to the Gnosh by three."

"I'll do the tally off the database," Bren said, tossing them a folder and swiveling her chair to face her computer. "And you guys count what you have there and what's left in that folder."

For a few minutes, all that could be heard was the sound of rustling paper and Bren's pen tapping the glass on the computer screen.

"Uh-uh," Maya moaned. "I hate to say this, but if my count is right, we've got a major problem."

Bren turned slowly in her chair. "We've got a problem all right," she agreed flatly. "A HUGE ratio issue. My figures show that girls outnumber boys two to one."

"Now what?" Morgan asked.

"Simple. We're done unless we get some more guys," Maya answered. "The way it is right now, every boy who signed up is going to get a million matches, and some of the girls won't get any."

The last part brought Amber to her feet. "Whoa! Wait! Not get any matches? After all this?"

"I don't like it any better than you do, girl," Maya said. "But facts are facts."

Bren jumped from her chair and grabbed a handful of blank questionnaires from the desk and another of flyers from the bookcase.

"Sitting around here whining about it isn't going to help," she cried as though about to enter a battlefield. "We've got to do something. Now. It's Saturday. The softball team has a game this afternoon. There's a boys' lacrosse match. And the track team always runs the streets around the school on Saturday morning. We'll divide and conquer."

"Now?" Maya whined. "I wanted to go to that art festival at the library, and while we're uptown, I thought we could all go grab a salad . . . "

"Forget it!" Bren snapped. "This is no time for fun. Maya, you'll have to drive us to school. You take the lacrosse match. Jamie, you hit the baseball game. Amber, you do a quick lab check—and walk the halls, too. There are always clubs meeting on weekends. Morgan and Alex, get to the Gnosh on foot and pick up any strays you can find there. I'll go after the runners."

She grabbed a sweater off the couch, tied it around her neck, and headed out the door.

Her recruits followed, Alex and Morgan tromping across the front yard toward the restaurant, and everyone else climbing into Mr. Beep. Usually, Bren was more than happy to squeeze in back, but today—without even calling "shotgun"—she claimed the passenger seat like a front-line general commanding the troops.

They pulled around the circular driveway and onto Oak Street, where they could see the younger girls starting to cut across the Deer Creek golf course.

"We'll meet you at the Gnosh at three," Maya yelled to them from the car window as they drove Mr. Beep away.

"Park in the front lot," she ordered Maya when they reached the high school. She hurriedly handed each girl a stack of forms and kept the remainder for herself. "Remember," she instructed, "flyers if they've got e-mail, questionnaires if they don't."

"There's Raj Chowdhury! He is too fine!" Maya cried, hopping out of the car. "Hey, Raj, wait up." She locked Mr. Beep and charged across the parking lot after the wiry lacrosse player, leaving Jamie, Amber, and Bren in her dust.

"That's the spirit!" Bren said approvingly. "Okay—go!"

Bren took off across the lot to the sidewalk. She stopped and looked in both directions. The track team had to be around here somewhere. Bren walked rapidly, stopping at every street to look up and down in search of the boys. By the time she'd covered six blocks, her feet felt like she was dragging barbells. She'd charged out of the house so fast she hadn't bothered to swap her pink espadrilles for her running shoes. Well, too bad—a girl had to do what a girl had to do. She set her mouth grimly and kept going. Finally, she spotted a few stragglers puffing down Cedar Street. One of them was Martin Johnson.

"Martin!" she hollered. "Wait up!"

Martin looked over his shoulder and nearly stumbled. "Can't stop!" he hollered back. "Catch up!"

Bren was wearing pink shorts and a white elbow-length T-shirt. Not too bad for running, though she'd prefer not to turn up at the Gnosh sweating like a glass of lemonade in August. The big problem was the pink espadrilles. Every step felt like the pavement was rising up to bash the soles of her feet. By the time she caught up with Martin, she was panting.

"Can't—you—guys—stop—for—a—minute?"

"Sorry!" Martin replied. "Coach will blow a gasket if he finds out we were standing around talking to a girl!"

"You want to talk to us, you gotta run with us!" his long-haired teammate added. He grinned at her, exposing a mouthful of braces with black bands.

"Did—you—sign—up—for—computer—dating?" she asked the long-haired guy.

"Nope, but I wouldn't mind if your name's in the computer," he replied. *Great,* she thought. *The hippie likes me.*

"It's—in—there—and—my—friends'—too . . . We—need—more—guys!"

Up ahead, another clutch of runners crossed Cedar on Eastbrook, headed toward the park. Just before Martin's group turned right, Bren stuffed a questionnaire in the hippie's hand and jogged left on Eastbrook.

"Dudes—hey—slow—down!" she hollered.

Brandon and Greg looked over their shoulders and laughed when they saw her coming. Bren knew she wasn't the most graceful runner, but she was only interested in Brandon's and Greg's questionnaires. The whole group kept moving, but they all slowed their pace to allow her to catch up.

"I—need—your—help!" she wheezed. Her face and lungs burned, but it was nothing compared to her feet. Pain sizzled along her soles and a blister burned into her left heel. Silently thanking God that they'd hung a left before the Gnosh, she jogged up alongside them and made her case for computer dating.

"Okay, okay, we're there! Huh, Brandon?" Greg asked his friend. "We'll get the rest of the team for you too." Nods of agreement rippled through the small group.

"Sure," Brandon agreed, "and as many juniors as we can. But fix me up with a babe, Bren."

Bren thanked them, finally able to breathe and speak, and she sprinted ahead to talk to two seniors. "Hey! Wait up!" she yelled.

A dark green Jeep Cherokee drove slowly by. Bren turned her head—and locked eyes with Christopher Russell.

He gave her an amused smile and turned left at the corner. Bren stood staring dumbly after him. Greg, Brandon, and their teammates ran around her. A torrent of words and whistles cascaded over her, but she didn't hear them. Russ had seen her running down the street chasing the track team! She turned back around and forced her feet to move. Just then, the Jeep Cherokee pulled up next to her.

"Hey, you look like you could use a lift!" Christopher Russell called.

Bren gasped. She ran her hand through her hair. It was soaking wet and plastered to her head. For a second, she couldn't think. This was the moment she'd been waiting for, but now that it was here she couldn't decide what to do. She was hot and sweaty. She could barely walk. And she must smell like a truckdriver. She swiped at her face with the heel of her hand and limped over to the car.

"Th-thanks. I guess I could." She slid into the passenger seat and managed a smile.

Her heart was pounding through her chest. *I'm with Christopher Russell! We're in his car together!*

"So, where to?" he asked.

"Not far—the Gnosh," she mumbled, afraid to look at him. *I don't even have on any lipstick,* she thought. She clasped her hands tightly in her lap and stared out the window.

"The Gnosh it is then." He reached over and turned up the volume on the radio.

Techno music blasted through the Jeep, making it impossible to talk. Techno wasn't Bren's sound, but at least it kept her from having to make conversation. Her ability to form words felt about as accessible as her ability to walk.

At the Gnosh, he pulled up to the curb, slammed on the brakes, and lowered the volume on the radio. "Here you are."

"Thanks," Bren managed.

"No problem."

She started to open the door.

Russ laughed, a cool, polished sound that sent shivers down her spine.

"Hey, mind if I give you a little advice?" he asked.

"What's that?" She turned back to look at him, one hand on the door handle.

"Next time you want to catch yourself a guy—wear some sneakers."

Bren flew out of the car and into the Gnosh.

All of the TodaysGirls were in the back booth, gleefully sharing how many guys they'd signed up when she collapsed next to Amber like the last survivor of a nuclear holocaust.

"Bren! What's wrong?" Jamie asked, rushing over. She'd just started her shift and was tying on a white apron.

"It's too horrible!" Bren wailed. Tears sprang to her eyes. She blurted out the story, scrubbing at her eyes with both fists. Mascara smudged her hands and ringed her eyes like a raccoon's mask.

"What a creep!" Alex said when Bren finished.

"And you *like* this person?" Morgan asked with amazement.

"That was so—so—" Amber groped for the right word. "Unkind!"

"But you don't understand," Bren cried, sniffing loudly. "I looked like a total idiot. You know how funny I look when I run, and I was all sweaty, and I really was chasing guys in my espadrilles! How can I keep embarrassing myself in front of him? What am I gonna do?"

"You're going to order yourself a double hot-fudge sundae and forget about him," Maya said briskly. "Not even Brandon or Greg would say anything that shallow—at least not to someone's face."

Bren started to protest, but there was no use. Her friends were only trying to help, and she loved them for it. But they didn't get it. And they never would. Not until they fell in love too.

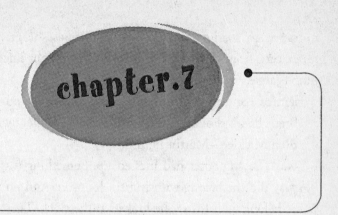

chapter.7

Bren watched anxiously as her high-speed laser printer zipped out the last page of matches. Greg and Brandon had more than lived up to their promise to sign up more guys. The final total had come in at 587 names, almost evenly divided between boys and girls.

Even before the printer stopped whirring, Bren began scanning the list for her friends' names. It was crazy, stupid, totally without sense—but she felt like she had to save herself for last. If she didn't, the match would not be Russ.

Quickly, she found Amber, Morgan, Maya, and Alex and jotted down their matches. Next came Jamie.

"Chandler, Chandler, Chandler," she muttered, her eyes sweeping down the long column of names. She found it and looked at the name across from it. "That can't be right," she muttered. A roaring sound filled her ears as she grabbed an index card from the desk and held it in a straight line, underlining Jamie's name and the one next to it.

Jamie Chandler—Christopher Russell. There was no mistake. Bren's hands shook as she searched the list for her own name. Bren Mickler—Martin Johnson.

No! The computer had messed up. Something was wrong. No way did she belong with Martin Johnson. And no way did Jamie belong with Russ. She looked at the clock. There was no time to redo the matches. She was supposed to be at the Gnosh in fifteen minutes to give her friends the names of their dates. She shoved the paper with everyone's match except hers and Jamie's into her pocket and ran downstairs.

"I'm ready, Mom!" she yelled. "I'll be in the car."

Bren went out to the garage and waited for her mother to come downstairs and take her to the Gnosh. She felt as though she'd been punched in the stomach. Jamie and Russ were already friends. Bren knew she'd never be happy with Martin Johnson, not even if he were the only guy on the planet. Quickly, she composed her face as her mother came into the garage and started the car.

"Bren? Are you all right?" Mrs. Mickler asked as she hit the remote for the garage door opener. "You look pale. You aren't getting sick are you?"

Bren shook her head no. She didn't trust herself to speak. She was sick all right. Heartsick. Lovesick.

At the Gnosh, a barrage of questions pelted her as soon as she slipped into the booth next to Amber.

"Who did I get?" Amber asked. "Did I get a writer?"

"Did you find somebody for me?" Morgan asked.

"You didn't hook me up with some artsy type, did you?" Alex demanded.

Bren took a deep breath. "You can't blame me for who you got," she cautioned. " I had nothing to do with it, remember? You want to blame somebody, you blame the computer."

"Oh, we know," Amber said. "Just tell us!"

Bren took the paper out of her pocket and slowly unfolded it. Out of the corner of her eye, she could see Jamie coming out of the kitchen with a tray of clean plates. She spotted Bren, set the tray on an empty table, and hurried over to the booth.

"So—do you have the verdict?" she asked. "Have I missed anything?"

"Bren's about to tell us!" Morgan cried.

"Good," Jamie said. "But hurry, I'm not supposed to be on break." She looked over her shoulder to gauge the whereabouts of Mr. Cross.

Bren swallowed hard. "Okay, here's what I have. Amber, you got Andy Love."

"*Love!*" Morgan squealed. "That's too funny! Did you hear that, Amber?"

Amber shrugged. "I have no clue who that is."

"Well, I have several clues," Maya said. "And one of them is that he's right here in this room." Her eyes danced. "I'll show you when Bren's done."

"Hurry *up*, Bren!" Amber pleaded, craning her neck to study the boys in the restaurant.

"Okay, okay. Morgan's next. Morgan, you're either going to love this or hate it. You got Jared."

Morgan grinned. Jared was her closest guy friend. They'd been hanging out together since they were little. "Whew! That's a relief! Dad said no dating, but Jared doesn't count."

"Alex, you got somebody named Randy Stetler."

Alex shrugged. "Thrill," she said, rolling her eyes.

"And Maya, you got Brandon Gallagher."

Maya blinked in obvious surprise. She'd already had some problems with Brandon and his sidekick Greg Muir. "Hmmmm, that could be interesting," she murmured, mulling it over. "Especially if he tries to redeem himself. You've got to admit it, though, he's a hottie."

"You won't get any argument there," Jamie agreed. She looked over her shoulder again. "Hurry, Bren! Tell me mine."

Bren set the paper on the table. She had two choices—tell the truth or stall. "Well, the thing is," she said slowly, "something went wrong with some of the matches. I have to rerun the last set, and there wasn't time before I left. So I don't have matches for you and me yet. Sorry."

"Bummer!" Jamie said cheerfully. "I gotta get back to work. But Bren, I need to talk to you before you leave, okay?"

Bren watched Jamie pick up the heavy tray and carry it over to the salad bar. She didn't want to talk to Jamie later. She wanted to dash out of the Gnosh, go home, and hide under the covers until it was time to leave for college. But of course she agreed.

"So where's my Prince Charming?" Amber demanded, gawking around the room.

Maya laughed. "Don't be so obvious! Look over at the counter. Third stool from the left. Shaved head. Eyebrow piercing."

Amber scanned, counted, then looked at her friends like she had a mouthful of lemon Warheads.

Maya laughed harder. "Maybe he *wants* to be a writer," she comforted her.

Bren giggled with her friends, but inside she felt tense, wired, like any second she could blast into orbit. What would she say if Jamie asked her what exactly had gone wrong with the computer? By the time Jamie's break rolled around, Bren's head hurt and she felt queasy.

"Hey, come over here for a second," Jamie called from the counter.

"Be right back," Bren told the others. She scooted out of the booth and over to where Jamie waited. Jamie looked wired too—and worried.

"What's up? Something wrong?" Bren asked, her temples pounding.

Jamie grabbed her arm and pulled her to the side of the room near the kitchen door. "Yes, or at least I think so. Last night I over-heard my mom on the phone with that Jack person. She said—and I quote—'it feels like the roof's caving in. I'm not ready to move that fast.' Something's wrong, Bren. Something terrible. I think she's going to lose her job right now—if she hasn't already. I'll just die if we have to move away!" Tears filled Jamie's eyes.

"Wait a minute! Wait!" Bren said. Her stomach did a flip. "Jamie, you don't know this for sure. You don't! You're only guessing. Why don't you just talk to her?"

Jamie sniffed. "I can't. She doesn't want me to know about it. I can't let on that I've been eavesdropping. But . . ." Jamie looked away and rubbed her eyes.

"But what?" Bren asked. "Is there some way I can help? Just tell me, and I will." She could have added, "It's the least I could do," but she didn't.

"*Would* you?" Jamie cried, turning back to face her. "That would be so great! Here's the deal. I heard her tell this Jack dude that she would meet him at Mario's tomorrow at seven. You know that restaurant at Third and Main with the green awning? Would you go over there with me?"

Bren blinked in surprise. "Go over there with you?" she echoed. "You mean—like waltz into the nicest place in town while they're having dinner?" *Well,* she thought, *if that's what it takes to make up for what I did—am about to do—for Jamie, it sure is the least thing I could do.*

Jamie managed a laugh. "No, of course not! I mean more like spy. I want to take a look at this Jack person. Something tells me he's the key to the mystery."

"Okay, sure. Of course I will. But come on over to the booth. Amber's having a meltdown over her date." Bren led the way, wishing for the luxury of a meltdown herself.

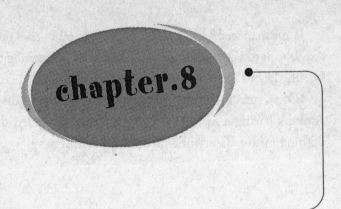

chapter.8

I *only have three choices,* she told herself the next morning. *A)* *Tell Jamie the truth, and let the matches remain as they are.* *B) Exchange the names, and tell Jamie she'd been matched with* *Martin, or C) Rerun the program.*

Both A and B were out, Bren decided. She couldn't live with the consequences. But if the computer actually spewed out her name with Russ's, that would be an entirely different situation. The important thing was not to overthink it. Quickly she called up her questionnaire on the screen and studied it. *What would it take to make it work,* she asked herself. But of course she knew. All she had to do was type "bowling" under favorite activities and "techno" under music, and she'd probably get herself a match.

It's not true though! It's a lie! You hate techno! And you don't even want to go bowling.

She closed her ears to the nasty little voice in her head. How could it possibly know for sure it wasn't true when she'd never been bowling in her life? Maybe she'd love bowling. Maybe she'd been born to bowl.

As spazzed-out as you are? Hah!

Okay, so she was no gazelle. But did that mean she couldn't bowl? All it took was a little dance step thing and a throw. How hard could it be?

Before the voice could protest again she typed in "bowling" and "techno," then hit *Enter* and reran the program. Then she squeezed her eyes shut and prayed while the new data was being processed. *Please, please, please make it work.* When the computer fell silent, she opened her eyes and scrolled rapidly down the screen.

Bren Mickler—Christopher Russell
Jamie Chandler—Martin Johnson

Yessssssss! It rolled Martin over to Jamie!! Bren hit the *Print* button and breathed a sigh of relief. She would give Jamie her match this evening when they showed up to spy at Mario's.

Mrs. Mickler dropped Bren off at the Gnosh at 6:45 P.M.—just enough time for Jamie and Bren to walk to Mario's. By the time they got there, Jamie's mom and the Jack dude would already be seated inside the restaurant. Jamie had to work till closing, but she had persuaded Mr. Cross to let her off one hour for "personal reasons."

Bren pushed open the door to the Gnosh, wondering whether to give Jamie her match before or after they went to Mario's. A romantic '50s song blaring from the jukebox stopped her in her tracks. Forced to inch past her, people were entering and leaving the restaurant, but Bren stood rooted to the spot like an ancient oak. The singer was singing, "Put Your Head on My Shoulder"! Just like in the poem that she'd read for English!

It had to be a sign. Mr. Cross had CDs from every era in his jukebox. Why would that particular song start the second she walked in the door? It must mean that everything would be all right! *Sure it will,* she told herself. All she'd done by rerunning the program was correct a computer error. *It'll be fine.* Bren exhaled with relief and walked into the dining area.

"Jamie! Hi!" she called.

Jamie whizzed out of the kitchen with a pair of cheeseburger platters, which she took to a back booth. "Gimme a sec," she whispered as she passed. "We're slammed tonight."

Bren reached in her pocket and touched the paper with the matches. *I'll show it to Jamie later,* she decided—after Mario's.

In about five minutes, Jamie came out of the kitchen wearing her navy blue nylon jacket. "Let's hit it," she said grimly.

The girls stepped outside and turned left on Eastbrook. It was a warm evening, just turning dark. Ordinarily, the pair loved walking at dusk. Tonight, though, a silent tension seemed to crackle off Jamie's skin with their every step.

"Come on, Jamie. Try to chill," Bren consoled when they turned left again at Main. "I know it's hard. There could be a million reasons why your mom is talking to this guy."

"Name one," Jamie countered. "Besides romance, of course. There's no way."

Bren thought fast. "Um—maybe your mom is just friends with him, and they're talking about *his* work and *his* roof caving in—not hers. Did you ever think of that?" Jamie didn't answer. They didn't say a word until they'd passed the park and crossed the busy King Street intersection that marked the beginning of Old Town Edgewood. Trendy coffee shops, bookstores, and restaurants lined the west side of the street, with stately older homes stretching along the east side, where the girls walked the last block before Mario's.

"Really, Jamie, think about it," Bren finally said. "This guy could be getting divorced or something, and your mom is just listening, just being a friend. Like me and Carl what's-his-name who moved away. He'd tell me all his problems, and I'd listen and tell him what to do. You know, most people don't realize what really good advice I can give sometimes, but that Carl guy did. He thought I was really intuitive, you know? And exceptionally people-smart. That's what he said. Exceptionally people-smart."

"Why am I laughing?" Jamie demanded. "I do NOT feel like laughing."

Bren grinned. "It must be because I'm so people—"

"No, you're not," Jamie said, grinning back.

The pair came to a sudden halt across the street from the restaurant.

"Okay, game plan?" Bren asked, looking around for Jamie's mom's car.

"We've got to get to the other side of the restaurant by the window," Jamie answered, pulling Bren by the arm to the corner of Third Street. They crossed the street hurriedly, and Jamie hid behind a tall topiary with tiny white lights beside the restaurant's huge plate-glass window.

"Okay, I'll stay here," Jamie whispered. "You look in the window. Mom's wearing a navy blue dress with a pink jacket."

"What do I do if she sees me?" Bren asked. She looked up and down the street again, but the coast was clear.

"Then wave and walk by," Jamie instructed from behind the tree. "I'll know what it means and go the other way. We can meet back at the Gnosh. Go!" She gave Bren a little push.

The window of Mario's restaurant was lettered in gold with the words "Mario's Fine Dining Since 1972." Bren pretended to read the menu displayed in the right corner while taking quick glances at the space between "Since" and "1972." She didn't see Ms. Chandler. She moved over a few more inches, studied the array of desserts, and looked into the larger space after "Mario's." Jamie's mom sat alone at a table peering at herself in the mirror of her compact.

"I see her," Bren intoned. "But no pink jacket. She's wearing a black sleeveless thing I've never seen before. And she's checking out her face."

"Whaaaaat?" Jamie squawked from behind the tree. "What would she do that for? Oh no! She's not crying, is she? Please tell me she's not crying."

Bren peered in the window again. Jamie's mom was smiling at a tall man who kissed her on the cheek and sat down opposite her at the table.

"Oh!"

"What? What is it?" Jamie cried, darting out from behind the tree.

"Get back!" Bren hissed. "You want them to see you?" The tall man had just taken Ms. Chandler's hand.

"Them? Who's them?" Jamie asked from the tree. "Bren, what is going ON?"

Slowly, Bren turned away from the window, took her friend's arm, and led her back across the street.

"Tell me, Bren," Jamie insisted. "I can handle it."

"Jamie, " she said slowly. "I hate to tell you this, but it's not money that has your mother all upset. It's romance."

Jamie stopped, open-mouthed. "No way! How do you know? You don't know!"

"I know," Bren said. "I even know who she's with. And you are not going to believe it."

"Who?"

"'Your mother sounds like a wise woman, Miss Chandler,'" Bren said in a deep voice.

"This isn't funny, Bren," Jamie cried. "You're joking, right? You can't really mean Mr. Bailey?"

"Oh yes, I can! Mr. *Jack* Bailey!" Bren crowed. "This is wonderful, Jamie! There's no terrible money problem, just romance. Maybe even love."

Jamie stuffed both hands into the pockets of her nylon jacket and picked up her pace. "I can't even wrap my mind around this," she said. "My mother hasn't dated since—since—since Dad left. This is too weird. Why does it have to be Mr. Bailey?"

Bren hurried to catch up. "That *is* the million-dollar question," she said. "But it's great! Love is wonderful."

Jamie didn't reply.

And again, the pair walked all the way past Edgewood City Park in complete silence, Bren's heart filling with an inexplicable joy for her best friend's lonely mother. As difficult as it was to keep her opinions to herself, Bren knew her silent-type friend well enough to quietly allow Jamie the space to digest the fact that her mom was dating their *teacher*. And Bren found a surprising feeling of hope rising up inside her. Hope for her own happiness. And hope that she could pull the whole thing off.

Jamie opened the door to the Gnosh and went inside with Bren at her heels.

"Jamie! You're back early!" Mr. Cross called from across the room. "I could use a hand over here."

"Gotta go," Jamie whispered. "But first—tell me who the computer matched us with. Did you get it worked out?"

Bren swallowed hard. Suddenly the hope was gone—stolen away by a single question. "Yeah," she answered with a shrug. "I got Russ and—you—you got Martin."

Jamie's eyes widened. "Johnson? I got Martin Johnson?"

"Yup. Weird, huh?" Bren said, making her best effort at a casual shrug. "Listen, Mr. Cross is staring at us. I'll catch you later." She turned and fled into the welcoming dark of the street before Jamie could ask any more questions.

chapter.9

On Monday, Bren logged on to the TodaysGirls.com site and typed in her password. She'd been with her mother since school got out, attending the Dior retrospective opening at the fashion museum at the college. It was 5:00 P.M., and everyone was waiting for her. As soon as she gained access, they pounced on her like a pack of feral cats.

> **faithful1:** r u sure the computer was working when u ran my name?
>
> **TX2step:** Where did u find this guy? He wants 2 take me 2 a Disney movie. I do NOT do cartoons.
>
> **nycbutterfly:** Brandon called me. 4get what I said B4. This is not going 2 work! JMO, but this idea is not so kewl

Bren sighed and slowly typed in her reply:

chicChick: Is anybody happy?
jellybean: I am
chicChick: oh bean ur always happy. what about you,
rembrandt?
rembrandt: Martin is not BF material, but I'm ok. I saw
Russ & told him to call u

Bren glanced at the phone on her desk and noticed the green
message light was blinking. She typed in a quick "BBS," took a
deep breath, and hit the message button.

"Bren?" the voice said.

"Yes!" she whispered aloud. "Yes, yes!"

"Uh, your friend Jamie tells me I got your name in that computer dating thing. So if you maybe want to go bowling Friday
night, I'll reserve us a lane. You don't have to call me back unless
it won't fly. Otherwise—I'll see ya about seven."

His voice sounded flat, like he couldn't care less whether she
could go. Bren felt her heart plummet to her feet. He didn't even
say if he was picking her up or she was supposed to meet him at
the bowling alley. She sat for a second, staring out the window.
This wasn't the way she'd planned it at all. *But maybe that's just
the way he is,* she thought. Not everybody performed vocal gym-
nastics like she did when they were excited. *Yes, that has to be it,*
she told herself, turning back to the computer.

chicChick: Russ was on answering machine. i gotta date!
rembrandt: 2 kewl!
faithful1: u ok? nervous?

Bren paused and considered that.

chicChick: yeah, but i'll get over it.

At least I hope I do, she thought as she logged off.

The next morning at swim practice, Jamie rushed over to Bren as soon as she—late as usual—stepped into the pool area.

"Guess who called me last night?" she bubbled. "Russ! He wanted to know if my date and I wanted to double with you guys Friday night. I told him I'd check with Martin, but I wanted to see if it was okay with you first."

Bren adjusted her suit and tried not to catch Jamie's eye. The last thing she wanted was a double date with Jamie and Martin.

"Did you tell him who your date is?" she asked. "That might change his mind in a hurry!"

Jamie frowned. "*Bren!* That's not fair. Martin's a nice guy. I like him. Maybe not boyfriend material, but still . . . I'm going to have fun Friday night. What do you want me to tell Russ?"

Bren shrugged. "I don't care. Tell him that's fine. Are we meeting him or what?"

Jamie glanced away toward the pool. "Um, he wanted me and

Martin to pick you up on the way. Something about the Jeep being in the shop and his brother dropping him off at the lanes."

"Fine. Whatever," Bren replied. "Listen, I gotta go warm up. We'll talk later." She looked longingly at the door to the locker room. Tears pricked her eyeballs like needles. He wasn't coming to pick her up! He hadn't even called her to talk over plans—he'd called Jamie! And now he wanted to double with Jamie and Martin so he wouldn't have to be alone with her! She walked over to the deck of the pool and started her stretches, swallowing hard.

"Hey, is something wrong?" Maya asked, coming up behind her. "I saw you talking to Jamie, and you looked like you'd lost your best friend. There's nothing wrong, is there? Is everything okay with Jamie's mom?"

Bren straightened up and made a show of stretching her neck muscles. "Yeah, everything's fine." Jamie had sworn Bren to secrecy about her mom and Mr. Bailey. "We were just working out plans for our dates. We're going to double."

"Double?" Maya sounded surprised.

"No big deal," Bren said, stretching away from Maya. "The problem is I don't know how to bowl. Do you?"

"A little." Maya laughed and wrinkled her nose. "Believe me, I'm no Diana Teeters."

"Who's she?"

Maya grinned. "Never mind. From what I hear, the thing with bowling is to get the right fit on the ball. You need the heaviest one you can handle. The footwork is pretty easy though. Watch." She held an imaginary ball in front of her, swung it back, and rolled low while her feet did a one-two-three step. "Try it."

Bren took four awkward steps and ended up with the imaginary ball behind her when it was time to roll.

"Bren! Maya! Just what sport do you think we're practicing in here?" Coach Short hollered. "Get in gear please!"

Maya wrinkled her nose at Bren again and led the way to the edge of the pool. At the starting signal, Bren plunged into the water and thrashed like a drowning cat. But by the time the race ended she felt better. The problem was that Russ didn't really know her yet, she decided. He and Jamie had class together—of course he felt more comfortable calling Jamie. Once they actually had a date, everything would be fine. She'd even get the hang of bowling—somehow.

On Friday evening, she examined herself carefully in the mirrored door of her closet. Crisp white Capris and a striped sweater in vivid crayon-box hues highlighted her dark coloring and showed off her slim figure. She smiled as she slipped into her new red flats. *Look out, Christopher Russell,* she thought, *it's just a matter of time . . .*

Headlights from a vehicle turning into the drive sent her flying down the stairs. "Bye Mom! Bye Dad! I'm outta here. Back by eleven!" she called from the foyer. Before anyone could answer, she ran out the door and onto the front steps. A dented brown van idled in the driveway. Bren squinted at it just as Jamie stuck her head out the front passenger window and hollered, "Hey! It's us!"

Bren couldn't answer. The van was a clunker—a total pile of junk. Martin Johnson was driving it. And—worst of all—white letters along the side read, "Patty's Pet Parlor, Where There's No Such Thing as a Mutt."

"Hurry up! What's wrong?" Jamie called.

"Nothing!" Bren pasted a smile on her face and headed down the drive. If a fairy godmother would appear right this instant she'd ask for only one wish—to wake up in her own bed facing nothing more terrible than the shrilling of the alarm clock. What would Russ think when she pulled up in *that* contraption?

The side door of the van slid open, and Jamie's younger sister Jessica popped her head out. "Bren! Mom's got a date tonight, so I get to go too!" she called. "Isn't that cool?"

Oh yeah, cool. "It sure is," Bren lied. She stepped up and swung herself onto the stained cloth seat beside Jessica, trying hard not to think about how the fabric might have gotten that way and what it might do to her white Capris.

"Hi, Bren," Martin greeted her. "Looking good, as always."

"Thanks," Bren murmured.

"Martin gave Jamie some candy," Jessica announced. "I already ate mine. You want one, Bren?" She held out a small box of foil-wrapped chocolate circles.

Bren shook her head no. Suddenly a hard lump formed in her throat. *I could just cry,* she thought, surprised. *I could break down and howl at the moon like a coyote. Why do I feel like this? Because geek-wad Martin gave Jamie chocolates? How stupid is that?*

All the way to Bowling World, she blinked back tears. But the second she spotted Russ slouched against the exterior brick wall of the bowling alley—wearing khakis and a honey suede jacket—Martin and his cheap drugstore chocolates flew out of her mind. A hottie like Russ up against a geek like Martin was like comparing Gucci to BargainLand. When the engine stopped, she hopped out of the van and hurried over to him.

"Hey! Been waiting long?" she called.

Russ looked past her to where Jessica was loudly asking Jamie and Martin the difference between a strike and a spare. "Who's the little kid?" he asked.

Bren wrinkled her nose. "I know—it wouldn't have been my first choice either," she whispered. "It's Jamie's little sister. Jamie's baby-sitting."

Russ's perfectly chiseled lips frowned. "Then we're getting our own lane," he decided. "I can't stand bowling with little kids. Tell Jamie whatever you want. I'm going in to see about another lane." He opened the door, went inside, and let the door close in her face, leaving her standing out front alone.

"He's getting us our own lane," Bren announced when Jamie and Martin joined her.

Jamie frowned and glanced at Martin who returned the expression. Bren ignored them. Jamie could think whatever she wanted, Bren decided, opening the door. *But the fact is,* she told herself, *Russ and I are on a date—and real dates don't include little kids.*

Inside, the noise was deafening. Bren stood uncertainly by the door and looked around. She saw Russ at the counter handing money to a balding man wearing a white T-shirt with a deer head on the front.

"What size shoes you need?" Russ asked as she came up.

"Shoes?" Bren looked down at her red flats, confused.

"Bowling shoes."

Behind the counter, rows and rows of the world's ugliest shoes were stacked like the bodies of foot soldiers. Bren stared at them, her heart pounding. She was going to have to actually stick her own feet in a pair of shoes used by strangers! Who knew what germs were in there?

"Sss-i-x," she stuttered.

The man in the white T-shirt swooped a pair of tricolored shoes off the shelf and plopped them down in front of her. "There you go. Size six, ladies."

Bren picked up the red, black, and yellow shoes and looked around desperately. Nobody had said anything about used shoes. She didn't have any socks and no way was she going to put her bare feet in those disgusting things without socks. They probably wouldn't even let her. There was probably some sort of law like at the shoe store. Quickly, she scanned the room for Jamie and saw her at the end of the long counter claiming a pair of brown and red shoes.

"Excuse me a second, Russ," she said, leaving the shoes on the counter. She ran over to Jamie. "You've got to help me," she whispered, grabbing Jamie's arm. "I don't have any socks with me. What am I going to do?"

Jamie looked down at Bren's feet in the red flats and groaned. "Oh, Bren, I don't believe this."

"Well, believe it," Bren snapped.

Jamie thought for a second. "Wait! Let me go ask Martin."

"What's the holdup?" Russ asked behind her. "Are we going to bowl or stand around talking all night?"

Bren whirled around.

"Uh—bowl," she said quickly. "I forgot my socks, but it's not a problem."

"Well grab a ball then and come on." He strode off toward the lanes.

Bren picked up the ugly shoes and went to find a ball. They all looked like giant cannonballs. She stuck her fingers in the holes of a small one and hefted it up. Her shoulder dropped six inches. She tried another. The holes were too large. The third one felt vaguely greasy. Finally, she settled on a pink ball with little sparkles embedded in it.

"Here you go," Jamie said, smiling sheepishly as she held out a pair of white tube socks.

"No way," Bren hissed at her friend.

"Bren," Jamie snarled uncharacteristically, "I went all the way to the van to get these. You're lucky Martin even had his gym bag with him! Get over it." Bren exhaled unhappily and took the socks—which at least were clean—from Jamie.

By the time Bren caught up with Russ, he was already changing his shoes. She sank into a chair beside him and pulled on the ugly tube socks. Maybe she could sort of roll up the material and keep it low around her ankle, she thought. Anything was better than pulling them up to her knees.

"You can go first," Russ offered when she had both shoes tied. Martin's socks looked like a pair of little white rubber inner tubes around her ankles.

"Uh, that's okay," Bren muttered. "You go."

"No—go on," he insisted. "I'll keep score."

Out of the corner of her eye, she could see Martin, Jamie, and Jessica three lanes over—they were all laughing. Bren picked up her ball and walked to the edge of the lane. She looked to her right and watched the woman in the next lane. She did a little run, lunged forward on one knee and rolled. When she finished, one leg kicked out behind her and both arms spread wide like she was ready to take flight.

Bren swallowed hard, backed up, and held the ball in front of her. Clearly, the trick was to aim for the middle and line up the ball with the one pin that stood in front by itself. She took a careful step, stopped, and swung the ball behind her. Two steps to go. One. Two. She ended with both feet together and the ball in front of her.

"Haven't you ever bowled before?" Russ asked behind her.

"Of course I haven't," she said over her shoulder. Then she leaned forward and drop-rolled the ball. Her position was too high. The ball took a lazy journey down the polished wood toward the front pin. And stopped cold.

"Whaaaat?" Russ squawked. "Oh, man!"

"It's okay, I'll get the hang of it," Bren said quickly. "I'll go get it." Before Russ could stop her, she stepped over the line onto the shiny wood.

"What are *do*ing? Are you nuts?" he hollered.

Too late. Bren crashed like a tower of blocks. She tried to get up, but it was like dancing on banana peels. She pulled herself to her hands and knees and prayed for Jamie to rescue her.

"What's the matter with you?" Russ demanded, looming over her. "You could break an arm pulling a stunt like that."

Bren crawled off the wood and allowed him to pull her up to her feet. Her face felt just hot enough to fry bacon on.

"Bren, are you okay?" Jamie yelled, running over with her face full of concern. "I saw you go down, and there was nothing I could do. Never, ever step over the line."

"You want to come sit down?" Martin asked. He took her arm and guided her to a chair. "Here, drink some of my soda. You're not hurt, are you?"

Russ picked up a ball and took his turn. A strike! Bren blinked back tears and watched him leap for joy as all ten pins crashed. He was so handsome. So graceful. So sure of himself. And she loved him with all her heart. She dug her nails into the side of Martin's Styrofoam soda cup and took a deep breath. Even if she couldn't bowl like a pro, she could at least be a good sport and try again.

By the evening's end, Bren had scored a grand total of 16 points. After the second game, Martin suggested that they all go to the Gnosh.

"Yes, let's!" Jamie agreed. "Is that okay with you guys?"

"I'd love to," Bren said quickly. Maybe if they could get out of this foreign environment, things would improve. It would be much easier to be herself where she felt comfortable.

Russ shook his head. "Can't. I was hoping maybe you could drop me off at home, actually. I—uh—got some stuff to do."

"But it's only nine-thirty," Jamie protested.

Bren swallowed hard and looked away. "Actually, I need to get home too," she said. She sat down and untied the hideous shoes. "Can you take me home too, Martin?"

"Sure," Martin said. He started to say something else, glanced at Russ, and obviously changed his mind.

Outside, Bren took a huge gulp of the cool night air. She felt like she was drowning. She glanced over at Russ. The impatient set of his mouth told her that he couldn't wait to get home.

All the way to Bren's house, Jessica chattered nonstop about her bowling score and what she was going to order at the Gnosh.

Bren stared out the window. She could feel Russ's boredom as though it were a sixth person in the van. Almost before Martin came to a stop, she popped her seat belt, opened the door, and jumped down.

"Good night, everybody," she said quickly. "I'll call you tomorrow, Jamie."

Martin turned around in his seat. ""Good night, Bren. I hope we can do something again sometime. Russ, I'll wait while you walk Bren to the door."

Russ's chiseled composure dissolved. "Oh—uh—yeah," he mumbled. "Just give me a minute." He climbed out of the van behind Bren and followed her up the drive to the house.

Normally, the porch lights next to the front door would be on when she came home from a date, but her parents weren't expecting her back so soon. Bren felt a rush of gratitude that Martin's headlights and the single lamp burning in the unused living room provided the only light. The thought of Russ seeing her wet eyes was almost more than she could stand

"Well, thanks," she said. "Maybe . . ." She stopped. Maybe what? Maybe he would ever want to go anywhere with her again?

"Listen—uh, Bren," Russ jammed his hands in the pockets of his jacket and looked down at the brown cobblestone of the steps as though they were microbes squiggling under a microscope lens. "I, uh—won't be calling you again."

Bren felt her insides collapse. She hadn't really thought he would after the disastrous date. But hearing it out loud in actual words felt like a splash of ice water in her face.

He rubbed his foot back and forth across the bottom step and didn't meet her gaze. "The thing is, I wouldn't even have gone on this date if I hadn't promised Jamie. Nothing personal. It's my dad. He'd have a cow if he ever found out I dated somebody who wasn't even American."

chapter.10

Completely speechless for the first time in her entire life, Bren opened her front door and went into the house. She climbed the stairs almost in a fog. She went into her room, closed the door, and sat down very carefully on the edge of her bed. Russ was prejudiced. He'd blamed it on his dad, but the same ugly bigotry filled him, too, or he never would have said it. Wrapping her arms around herself, Bren rocked back and forth as hot tears slid painfully and silently down her face.

Love is not rude, is not selfish . . .

Love is not happy with evil, but is happy with the truth.

Lines from Jamie's reading floated through her brain. They were disjointed and out of sequence. But they all brought her to the same place—the truth. Christopher Russell looked perfect on the outside, but inside he was as hollow as a Ken doll.

"Bren? Honey? Is that you home so early?" Mrs. Mickler poked her head around the door, took one look at her daughter's face and flew across the room.

"Oh, Mommy!" Bren sobbed, throwing herself into her mother's arms. She blurted out the story of the date, stumbling when she came to the part where Russ revealed his bigotry. She didn't want to hurt her mother too.

Mrs. Mickler smoothed back her daughter's hair. "I'm so sorry," she whispered into it. "I know how much it hurts. Believe me, I know . . . Right now there's a part of me that wants to go after that boy and give him a piece of my mind. But it wouldn't do any good because it's how he's been raised. All we can do is pray that someday, something will happen to show him the truth."

"But I loved him, Mom!" Bren wailed.

"I know that's how it felt," Mrs. Mickler said. "Attraction is a powerful thing. It hits you like a ton of bricks and makes it hard to think straight sometimes. But honey, attraction can leave just as fast as it arrives. Real love stays steady and true. When love comes, I promise you it won't be like this. Come downstairs with me now and have some cocoa, okay? You'll feel better."

Bren managed a shaky smile. Cocoa was her mother's answer to everything from skinned knees to broken hearts. But she allowed herself to be led down the curved staircase and into the kitchen. The phone rang, and the mother and daughter exchanged a silent glance of understanding as the answering machine picked up.

She could return her friends' concerned calls in the morning. Emotionally drained and physically exhausted, Bren wasn't ready to tell them just *how* badly the date had really ended. Right now, all she wanted was to be fed hot chocolate and Oreo cookies like she was five again.

The next morning she woke tired and puffy-eyed. She stumbled out of bed and logged on to the TodaysGirls site. Already, her friends were in mid-chat about the disastrous fall—including Martin's horrible socks—and her awful date that ended early. *Just wait till they find out how awful,* she thought. They must've seen her name when she gained access, because the chat immediately stopped.

  faithful1: u ok?
  chicChick: yeah.
  jellybean: I keep telling you he's a creep. u can do better. nothing is better.
  nycbutterfly: that's right. don't sweat it--it's over
  rembrandt: he just wasn't 4u.
  chicChick: That's 4 sure! I should have let u have him when u got him

Bren gasped as soon as she hit *Enter*. Her friends' concern had brought all the bad feelings rushing back. She had typed fast without thinking, and now the truth stood there in harsh online print. She had deceived Jamie. Again, there was a long pause on the screen. Bren put her hands over her face and moaned.

rembrandt: what do u mean?

Bren didn't reply. What could she possibly say? And how could she spill out her heart about Russ now? She was about to lose every friend she had.

rembrandt: WHAT DO U MEAN????
faithful1: r u saying jamie got matched to russ and u changed it?
nycbutterfly: girl, I hope u wouldn't do a thing like that. Did u get martin, 2? We do not btray each other 4 guys or lie to each other!!! Talk, bren.

Tears flooded Bren's already burning eyes. It was true. There was an unspoken pact that their friendship came before any guy. But . . . this was different. This was love. Or what had seemed like love anyway.

chicChick: i only changed 2 things in the questionnaire. u no how bad i wanted to go out with him. please, please, please understand!

Bren waited through another excruciating pause for their response to her totally selfish actions. Then suddenly, their comments flashed onto the screen rapid-fire.

> **rembrandt:** I do NOT understand. not so long ago, bren,
> u blamed me 4 b-traying u. and I hadn't—but u did it
> 2 me! 2 ur best friend!!
> **faithful1:** what were u thinking???
> **nycbutterfly:** bren! How could u?
> **TX2step:** U blew it big time.
> **jellybean:** it wasn't even worth it.

That was for sure. Bren logged off. There was no sense trying to defend herself. Nobody wanted to listen or understand. The rest of the weekend dragged like a health class, only without the comfort of being able to switch off her mind. Over and over, Russ's last words to her ran through her mind. She never wanted to speak to him again. And repeatedly, Bren practiced apologizing to Jamie, but she couldn't bring herself to log back on or pick up the phone.

For the first time in her swimming career, Bren arrived early for practice, just as the janitor opened the front doors. She tromped to the locker room and suited up. Glancing at the clock, she realized no one would be in for at least half an hour and wished she'd brought a magazine. But suddenly, the door to the pool area opened and closed, and Jamie's voice echoed back to the locker room. *She must be here to help Coach,* Bren thought as she stood up, her heart pounding in anticipation as Jamie bounded in.

"Oh," Jamie said, spotting Bren. She turned around to leave.

"Wait!" Bren cried. "I need to talk to you. Let me explain . . ."

Jamie turned back. "There's nothing to explain," she said evenly. "You did what you did. All you cared about was yourself. Well, I have a news flash for you. Not only did it not work, but Russ called me yesterday and we went to a movie. As a matter of fact, he's picking me up after work tonight, too."

Bren's eyes widened.

Love is not jealous. The words banged around in her brain as she fought down a strong surge of envy.

"Jamie, listen to me," she begged. "Russ is not how he seems. He's—"

"Save it," Jamie snapped, glaring as she pulled the brim of her White Sox cap down over her eyebrows. "Just because you two didn't hit it off doesn't mean it won't work for us. We have a lot in common, and we're getting along great, for your information."

"But you don't understand . . ."

"Oh, I understand all right," Jamie said. "First you betray me, and now you're jealous and want to wreck everything."

"I don't," Bren said miserably. "Honest, I don't! Jamie, something happened Friday night. When Russ walked me to the door he said he wouldn't be calling me again because—because of his father. At least he said it was his father, but the truth is he and his father are both prejudiced. He's a bigot, Jamie." Tears rushed to Bren's eyes.

For a second Jamie looked startled. But she whirled around and pulled open the door. "Nice try," she said. "At least you're creative." The door slammed behind her.

Bren slumped back on the bench and tried to breathe. Things kept getting worse and worse—and all because she thought she was in love. And Jamie wouldn't even listen to the truth. She could hear voices approaching from outside. Quickly, she stood up and pulled her towel out of her gym bag. The door opened and Maya, Amber, Morgan, and Alex came through, laughing and talking.

"Hey," Bren greeted them.

Nobody answered. Morgan managed a weak smile and a wave.

Bren took her suit and went into a stall to change. When she came out, everyone was already heading out to the pool.

"Wait, you guys," she called after them, "can I say something please?"

"What?" Maya asked, turning back. "You need to forget about this guy."

"Did Jamie tell you what he said to me? Did she tell you he's a big, fat racist pig?" Bren asked.

"What are you talking about?" Amber asked.

"I'm talking about Mr. Christopher Romeo Russell telling me I wasn't even an American," she replied. Shock flitted across

Maya's face. Amber looked sick and Morgan's mouth formed a perfect "O."

"Explain why we should believe you after what you did with the computer dates?" Alex demanded.

Bren looked her straight in the eye without flinching. "Because I'm telling the truth," she said quietly. "What I did was wrong. I know it and I'm sorry. If I could undo it, I would. All I can do now is try to save Jamie from getting hurt. Russ is not a nice guy, and Jamie refuses to believe it."

Maya sighed. "If that's true we've got ourselves one big problem then."

Amber nodded. "Jamie's exactly where you were with Russ last week, Bren," she said. "She thinks she's fallen in love."

chapter.11

Bren tried all week to talk to Jamie, but Jamie was like a windup racecar. When she wasn't rushing off to the Gnosh or speeding down the hall to avoid Bren, she was with Russ. The first time Bren saw them walking hand in hand to his car after school, a flood of emotion washed over her. Jealousy. Pain. Fear. Mostly fear. Everything in her screamed that this was not a good place for Jamie to be.

On Friday, she slid into her seat next to Jamie in English. As always since their fight, Jamie turned her body away so that Bren looked directly into her left shoulder. Bren sighed and opened her poetry book. She missed Jamie so much—it was like waking up one morning and finding herself without a hand or a foot. But Jamie didn't seem to miss her at all.

"People! In your seats please!" Mr. Bailey shouted. "Every day it's taking longer and longer to get down to business. We have to finish this unit before finals and we've got a long way to go."

When the din subsided, he held up two essays, one in each hand.

"We have been studying the various ways poets have written about love through the ages," he said. "Particularly the Romantic poets. Today I have chosen two of you to reread your selections for us, so we can compare and contrast romantic love with the love one feels for friends, family, and others. What are the similarities? What are the differences? And how are those differences reflected in the language the poet uses?"

His gaze turned to the right side of the room.

"Bren. Jamie. Will you come up here, please?"

Bren looked over at Jamie, but Jamie refused to return her gaze. She stood up, strode to the front of the room, and took her paper from Mr. Bailey. Bren followed, wishing she didn't have to read her poem. It felt weird reading about romantic love after she'd just been dumped.

"You go first, Bren," Mr. Bailey said.

She took her paper, read it in a flat tone, and returned to her seat. Jamie cleared her throat and read hers slowly, with much more feeling than she'd used the first time.

"'I may speak in different languages of men or even angels.'" She paused and looked straight at Bren. "'But if I do not have love, then I am only a noisy bell or a ringing cymbal.'"

A surge of heat crept up Bren's neck. Jamie was telling her

that all her protests about Russ were nothing more than a loud annoyance. She looked away and caught Martin staring at her. Did he think the same thing? Had Jamie told him what had happened? If she had, well, whatever. What Martin Johnson thought about anything was no concern of hers.

"'Love is patient and kind,'" Jamie was saying. "'Love is not jealous, it does not brag, and it is not proud.'"

The word *jealous* flew at Bren like darts. She stared at her desktop. Okay, it was true. Part of her *was* jealous of Jamie and Russ's relationship. It's not that she wanted Russ to be her boyfriend anymore. She'd seen him for what he was, but a part of her still longed to fall in love. The dizzy excitement filled life with sparkle and expectation. Now that it was gone, everything seemed flat and gray.

Jamie finished reading and returned to her seat. She reached down to the floor for her bag, took something out, and slipped it into the front of her book. Bren didn't see what it was, but she could feel Jamie's tension. She was as charged as a new battery. Whatever it was that was going on inside her was building up to an explosion. As soon as the bell rang, Bren grabbed her poetry book and started to stand up. She wanted as far away from Jamie Chandler as she could get. But before she got to her feet, Jamie reached over and slapped something down in front of her.

"Here! Take this!" she cried. "You need it a lot more than I do." It was the tasseled bookmark with the words from 1 Corinthians.

"Wait a sec—" Bren started to protest, but Jamie ran from the room.

People were staring at her. Bren picked up the bookmark and slipped it into her poetry book. She could feel their questioning eyes boring holes through her skin, but she refused to act like it bothered her.

"Hey, what was that all about?" Martin Johnson asked. He came over to lean against Jamie's empty desk.

"Nothing," Bren snapped. She stood up and picked up her own bag from the floor.

"Sure seems like a million years since we went bowling, doesn't it?" Martin asked. "So much has changed."

He sounded sad. Bren looked at him and shrugged. "Yeah, well. Stuff happens," she said. "I gotta go."

She stood up and walked past him out the door.

In the hall, she saw Maya standing at her locker. "Bren!" Maya called. "Come here! I've got news!"

Bren had hoped to go straight to her own locker, get her books for tonight's homework, and leave without having to talk to anyone.

"What's up?" Bren asked, hoping her face didn't betray her feelings.

Maya's dark eyes glowed. "I got us all dates! After our nasty computer dates, we deserve some fun."

In spite of herself, Bren felt a spark of interest. "Huh? How did you do that?"

"Well," Maya said with a grin, "I actually only got dates for you, me, and Amber. Morgan and Alex are too young. These guys are seniors."

"Are you sure they even want to go out with us?"

Maya opened her locker and made kissing noises at the picture of Denzel Washington taped to the back of the door. "That's the best part. They all three know who we are already! And they happen to think we're babes. Which, of course, we are."

Bren grinned. If Jamie were with them, it would be just like it used to be. "So who are they? How did it happen? Talk to me!" she ordered.

Maya took out a math book and a steno pad and shoved in a biology text. "Mine is Jason Azarian. And Amber has Raj Chowdhury, and you, my dear"—she waved the steno pad with a flourish—"have Bobby McClain."

Bren's jaw dropped. Bobby McClain was senior class president. He played first-string basketball and had a smile that could light up Los Angeles. "Are you kidding?" she squealed. "How did I get *him*?"

"He requested the pleasure of your company, that's how. He's calling you tonight. I gave him your number. Hope that's okay."

"Are you kidding? Thank you, thank you, thank you!" Bren shrieked. But then she remembered the betrayal that still lay in the middle of their group. "Maya? We've—uh—never really talked about what happened with Jamie and me, you know. I feel weird with it between us."

Maya nodded. "Come on, let's go sit in Mr. Beep. We can talk for a while, and then I'll take you home. Morgan is staying for Photography Club. That oughta last about a week." She rolled her eyes and wrinkled her nose.

The girls went outside and climbed into Maya's vintage Volkswagen Bug.

"You guys are all talking to me again," Bren said. "But there's all this unspoken stuff. I feel like you can't trust me now." Her voice cracked.

"What you did was rotten," Maya said. "It goes against every code of friendship in the universe. But you know that Bible verse Jamie had for poetry class? Amber posted it on the Web site, and it's all about where we went as friends. There's this one part that says, 'Love does not remember wrongs done against it.' We're supposed to forgive you. We all talked about it and decided that your head was majorly messed up, or you never would have done it."

"Yeah?"

"Yeah."

"But the big question is, can you trust me again?" Bren asked.

"I don't believe you'd ever do something like that if you were thinking straight," Maya answered. "The big question is—as I see it—are you thinking straight now?"

"Of course I am!" Bren answered. "I'm through with Russ."

"Good." Maya turned the key in the ignition, and the old car rumbled to life. "Because we need to concentrate on Jamie. She's in over her head and ignoring all of us—kinda like you were when you were riding that boat."

Bren nodded. "I know, but I don't know what I can do. Have you tried to talk to her? I told her what Russ said to me, but she didn't believe it. And today she slammed this on my desk and told me I need it more than she does." She reached in her book and pulled out the tasseled bookmark.

Maya glanced at it and shook her head. "We've talked to her. But we might as well have talked to the wall of the school. Brick listens better than she does."

"So what happens now?" Bren asked as they pulled out onto the street.

Maya shrugged. "I don't know. There's nothing we *can* do when she's never online and spends all her time with Mr. Wonderful. We can talk about it on the site later, though—we're meeting in the chat room at five, as usual."

For the first time in almost a week, Bren logged on at five sharp to find everyone but Jamie anxiously waiting.

jellybean: rembrandt is over the top.

faithful1: is it time 2 confront her?

nycbutterfly: mayB. But how? When?

chicChick: We need 2 b careful.

faithful1: u got that right. But if he is racist his values r not rembrandt's.

chicChick: mayB all we have 2 do is wait. mayB he will show his true self

TX2step: he hasn't so far and she's been with him every minute

chicChick: i say we give him some more time. he's bound 2 blow it

nycbutterfly: OK. but 1 week only. This is not kewl

faithful1: 1 week. I agree. Not kewlx2!!!!!!

nycbutterfly: hey, faithful1, your new date call?

faithful1: Yes! We r triple-dating. They have tickets 4 all of us 2 go 2 Phantom of the Opera!!

chicChick: 4 real?

faithful1: 4 real.

Bren started to type in another question when the shrill of the phone on her desk stopped her in mid-thought. She leaned over and picked it up.

"Bren?" a deep voice asked.

Her heart raced. It was Bobby McClain. She recognized his voice from the announcements he'd made on the PA system at school.

"This is Bren," she said coolly.

"Great. Listen, I hope it's okay that I have your number— Maya gave it to me—but I'd sure love it if we could get together Saturday night. My friends and I got tickets for a show, and I thought it might be fun. I know we don't know each other too well, but I've—uh—been admiring you and . . ."

Bren's heart turned a cartwheel. "I'd love to," she interrupted. "It's a great show. Who's driving?"

"Me," he replied. "I'm borrowing my mom's minivan, so we can all go together in the same car. How about if I pick you up at seven? Curtain's at eight. Maybe stop at the Gnosh afterwards?"

"Cool," Bren said. "I'll see you then."

She hung up and immediately started typing.

chicChick: Bobby McClain called. HE IS 2 KEWL!!!!!!!!
nycbutterfly: Slow down, girl!
chicChick: I'm slow! I'm slow!
TX2step: Slow as an x-press train
chicChick: This guy is the kewlest! u don't get it.
nycbutterfly: We get it that u need to take it EZ
chicChick: All right! U win!!

Bren logged off fifteen minutes later and ran to her closet. She had the perfect dress for a Saturday night at the theater—a short black sleeveless with a three-quarter-sleeve mesh cardigan embroidered with tiny pink and white flowers. All she needed to make it perfect were her black embroidered platform sandals, a black velvet hair band—and her best friend Jamie to share in this excitement.

chapter.12

Bren twirled in front of the mirror in her black dress. Her mind bounced from her upcoming date with Bobby McClain to Jamie, who was still not speaking to her. According to Maya, Jamie was going to a party tonight with Russ. She had even taken the night off from the Gnosh. Bren frowned. Jamie's art camp savings plan meant working every hour Mr. Cross would give her. The only way she'd give up extra cash was if she were too head-over-heels in love to think straight.

The sound of a car pulling into the drive jolted her thoughts back to the moment. Bren smoothed her dress and forced herself to remain in the living room until the doorbell rang. The sound of voices coming up the walk told her that everyone had piled out of the van and followed Bobby to the door. By the time the doorbell chimed, she was already smiling in anticipation.

"Hi, Bren," Bobby McClain greeted her. He looked down from his six-foot-something view and flashed her a shy smile. "You look great. I—uh—brought you these." He held out a bouquet wrapped in green florist paper.

Twelve pink carnations! Bren buried her nose in the flowers and breathed in their spicy scent. "Thank you, Bobby," she murmured. "That's so sweet! Come on in, everyone. Let me put these in some water and grab my purse."

"Isn't this cool!" Maya exclaimed as she drifted into the foyer in a cloud of Happy perfume. "I've been wanting to see this show forever!"

"Me too!" Bren agreed, thinking how awesome Maya looked in a simple aqua sheath with spaghetti straps.

"We have great seats," Bobby announced, smiling at Bren. "Center orchestra, sixth row."

"Then I'd better hurry," she murmured. Her heart pounded as she hurried into the kitchen. He'd spoken to her as though she were the only person in the house. In the world. In the universe. Bren hurriedly filled a tall ceramic urn with water, unwrapped the flowers, and stuck them into the vase in one bunch.

"I'm ready!" she announced, coming back into the foyer and grabbing her purse off the newel post. "Let's go!"

As her friends filed out the door, Bobby guided her toward it with one arm around her shoulders. Her mind reeled. *Could* this *be love? This is so different from the way it was with Russ.*

Maybe . . . No, she told herself firmly. Of course not. It was too soon for love. Whatever this dizzy feeling was though, she never wanted it to end.

In the kitchen the phone shrilled.

"Do you want to get that?" Bobby asked her.

Bren shook her head and smiled. "The machine will pick it up." Stepping into the open doorway, she breathed in the soft night air. It smelled like earth and rain and wonder all wrapped up in one beautiful package.

"Bren! Are you still there? Please, Bren, pick up! I need you!" a tinny voice sounded from the kitchen.

"It's Jamie!" Amber cried. "That's Jamie on the machine!"

Maya shot past Bren into the house and through the dining room with Bren at her heels.

"Don't hang up, Jamie!" Bren yelled. "Don't hang up!" She leaped in front of Maya and grabbed the phone. "Jamie? Are you there?"

"Bren? Oh, thank God you picked up! I need help! Please!" Jamie cried.

By now everyone was crowded around in the kitchen. Bobby stood beside Bren, one arm protectively around her shoulders again.

"Slow down," she said into the phone, "and tell me what's happening."

"I'm at this party with Russ," Jamie said. "We got here like an hour ago and—and—"

And Russ dumped her, Bren thought, her fear replaced quickly by annoyance. She rolled her eyes and glanced at the clock. If they were going to make curtain, they needed to leave this minute. If Jamie had a broken heart, it wasn't like she didn't know what she was getting into.

"Everybody is *drunk,* Bren!" Jamie cried. "Including Russ. I tried to call my mom, but she's out. And Maya left already. I know you're mad at me, and this is your big night, but please, *please* help me! I'm so scared, Bren! If somebody calls the police . . . There must be a hundred people here!" Her voice climbed two octaves.

Bren looked at her flowers on the counter, then up at Bobby's concerned face and felt something inside her crumble. This was so unfair! Finally, something good had happened to her, and Jamie was ruining it.

"Bren, are you there?" Jamie screeched. "Please, Bren! I know I don't deserve your help. I've been so—" Her voice cracked and broke into a torrent of sobs.

Bren took a deep breath. "I'm here. Just tell me where you are."

"It's five-sixteen McCaulay Avenue. Hurry! Please, please, hurry!"

Slowly, Bren replaced the receiver. "I can't go with you tonight, Bobby," she said. "I have to help my friend. She's in trouble."

"I'm all over that," Maya cried. "Forget the phantom."

"What? Whoa! Wait a minute!" Jason cried. "It doesn't take three people to pick up one."

120

"Yes, but Jamie's our friend too," Amber said. "If she's in trouble, I wouldn't feel right if I went to the play."

Maya shook her head. "No, Jason's right. It's not fair to stick the guys with three tickets. Amber and Bren should go to the play. I'm the one with a car. I'll go get Jamie."

Jason and Raj looked visibly relieved. But Bren couldn't consider letting Maya drive off in Mr. Beep to a party full of drunks. Suddenly the memory of Jamie's standing in front of the class reading her verse flooded into Bren's mind. Jamie's voice filled her head like the bass of a rock song. "*If I do not have love I am nothing.*"

"No! You guys go to the show. I'm getting her myself. I need to." The decisiveness of her own voice amazed her.

Maya met her gaze and nodded. "Okay, then. But just how will you do it without a car?"

"Martin," she replied. "I'll call Martin Johnson."

chapter.13

I hate to leave you here," Bobby McClain said for the third time. "If I weren't the driver—"

"It's cool," Bren assured him. "Go. I'll be fine."

"I'll call you tomorrow."

Would he? Who knew? Sharp tears stung Bren's eyes like nettles, but she smiled and hurried everyone out the door. She ran to the phone book and looked up Martin Johnson's number. Her fingers shook as she dialed it. "Be home, Martin," she whispered. "Please be home."

He was.

"Sit tight," he told her. "I'll be right there."

Within moments, the ratty brown van pulled into the driveway. Bren ran out and climbed in. This time she didn't care about the stains on the seat or even the stupid sign painted on the side door. All she could think of was Jamie, scared and alone in a strange house where no one was in charge and everyone was out of control.

Martin knew McCaulay Avenue and got them there in ten minutes. But to Bren it seemed like ten hours. Now that she had decided to do this, Jamie's fear had become hers. She clenched her fists until her knuckles whitened.

"Looks like that's the house up ahead there to the right," Martin said as they pulled onto McCaulay. Cars jammed both sides of the street despite the "No Parking" signs. Loud techno music and excess teenagers poured from the old yellow and brown house like gravel from a dump truck. And in the center of it all stood Jamie on the bottom step of the porch looking like an abandoned puppy.

"Let me out right here!" Bren cried. "Go around the block and come back for us. There's nowhere to park."

She opened the door and jumped down off the high ledge of the van. Her black silk pantyhose caught on a sharp edge, but she ran, ignoring the ripping sound.

"Jamie!"

Jamie looked up, saw Bren flying down the sidewalk, and leaped off the porch step. They met in a hug at the end of the cracked concrete walk leading up to the house.

"Thank you!" Jamie cried into Bren's hair. "Thank you, thank you, thank you!"

"It's okay. Come on now. Martin's circling back for us." Bren took Jamie's hand, like they were back in Brownies, and led her past a swarm of losers laughing and throwing food and half-full paper cups at each other. Something cold and wet splashed on the arm of Bren's mesh cardigan. Immediately, the soured, yeasty smell of beer assailed her.

"Oh, Bren!" Jamie cried.

"It's okay," Bren said. She wiped it off with her hand and prayed for Martin to hurry.

"Jamie!"

A deep voice spun both girls around. Russ came down the steps toward them "Where you going? It's early," he slurred, glaring at Bren. "What are *you* doing here?"

"Taking my friend home," she replied. "She doesn't belong here."

"Oh yeah?" Russ demanded, putting his face into hers. The stench of alcohol soured his breath. "Says who? You aren't her boss."

Bren looked up into the glazed blue eyes that only two weeks ago had sent shivers down her spine. "No, but I'm her friend," she said evenly. "Come on, Jamie, there's Martin."

Martin's mother's ancient van crept down the street through the throng of cars and people and pulled to a stop. Bren let Jamie climb in front, then crawled into the backseat and slid the heavy door shut. She looked across the littered lawn at Russ's angry, contorted face and winced as they pulled away. How could she have ever confused what she'd felt for him with love?

"Let's go to the Gnosh," Martin suggested. "Jamie looks like she could use something to eat."

Bren yelped. "Are you kidding? I smell like sour beer! I've got to go home and change. If I walk in there like this Mr. Cross will be on the phone to my parents in a New York minute."

Bren saw Martin's quick grin in the rearview mirror. "Home it is then. Afterwards, we're noshing at the Gnosh. Hey, I hope that dress isn't ruined," he added as he turned onto the main street. "That sweater rocks with the dress, you know. Mesh is a perfect complement."

Bren grinned. Martin's fashion observations still amazed her. Suddenly she thought of something and got serious "Martin? I—uh—I owe you an apology. I've been kind of—" She groped for the right word.

"Cold?" he supplied.

A surge of heat rose from her feet. "Yeah, something like that."

"Forget about it. I know I'm not the average guy," Martin replied, laughing. "But just wait—to know me is to love me!"

"I'm sure! There's nothing I admire more than modesty!" Bren teased. Martin Johnson would never be a boyfriend, she thought, but he would be a friend—a good friend. The kind *that always trusts, always hopes, and always continues strong.* She winced again at the words from Jamie's Bible verse. Just two weeks ago when Ms. Chandler had shown them the tasseled bookmark, she'd actually thought they were romantic! They were about real love. *Strong* love.

At home, she took off the black dress and hung it on a hanger to take to the dry cleaners. It seemed like a million years since she'd put it on. She glanced at the clock. The first act wasn't even over yet. She pulled on a pair of the plain straight-legged jeans that Jamie preferred and a coral sweater and ran downstairs. Jamie and Martin had flipped on the TV and were watching an old movie.

"I love these old flicks," Martin said as she came into the family room. "It's *Love Story*. Come watch. It just started. Then we can go to the Gnosh and grab some food."

Bren sat down on the couch next to Jamie and let herself be drawn into the romantic tale of a gorgeous young couple who met when they were undergraduates at Harvard and Radcliffe, fell in love, got married, and lived happily ever after until the young wife got sick and died.

"Listen!" Martin said at the final scene. "This you gotta hear!"

Oliver, the young husband, was talking to his father-in-law. "Love," he said sagely, "means never having to say you're sorry."

"Would you believe *that* was the most famous line in the movie?" Martin crowed as the credits started rolling. "In 1970, it was plastered across America—posters, T-shirts, everywhere. Isn't that unreal?"

Jamie groaned and covered her face with a pillow. "I don't believe it! That is the sappiest thing I ever heard!" she moaned. "Not to mention totally untrue."

"You can say that again!" Bren agreed. "Jamie, I am sorry, sorry, sorry for everything."

"Me too," Jamie said. "I can't believe how stupid I was to fall for Russ's lines and not believe what you told me. I'll never forget what you two did for me tonight. Never." She grinned at both Bren and Martin and grabbed her stomach. "Now—please—feed me! I'm starving."

At the Gnosh, they ordered double cheeseburgers and chili fries. As soon as the server took their order, the door opened and Maya and Amber filed in with their dates while Bobby McClain held the door open for them. Bren had forgotten what Bobby had said about coming to the Gnosh! A quick, automatic surge of panic raced through her. What would he think when he saw her sitting in a booth next to Martin Johnson? Bobby was so cool, so popular, so . . .

He'll think you have made a great friend. And if he doesn't, too bad.

"Hey guys! Come join us!" she called. Who owned this firm new voice in her head? "We can push a bunch of tables together That okay with you, Martin?"

"Sure," Martin said, flushing with pleasure.

Bren jumped up from the booth and went over to Bo "I'm sorry about tonight," she said shyly. "But I had to Jamie. Martin—my friend Martin—and I got her out just in time. It was a zoo. I hope you understand."

Bobby McClain smiled down at her from six-feet-s

"Hey, you just did what any good friend would do. Don't worry about it. There'll be other nights."

Bren smiled gratefully. Bobby McClain cared about other people. He was just the kind of guy she wanted for a boyfriend. *I hope it works out,* she thought as she dragged two chairs over to the tables Martin and Jamie were shoving together. But even if it didn't, she knew she'd survive. She'd made a wonderful new friend tonight. In fact, counting Martin she'd made two of them.

Epilogue

chicChick: did last nite rock or what? maya--u have my permission to fix me up anytime!

faithful1: same here!! beats computer dating with a stick

nycbutterfly: ditto. we missed u @ phantom, chic!!

chicChick: missed u2. but feels good to be back on same team. right, rembrandt?

rembrandt: right.

jellybean: so ur friends, again?

chicChick: yeah.

rembrandt: the best

TX2step: ACK! I just had breakfast.

Net Ready, Set, Go!

I hope my words and thoughts please you.
Psalm 19:14

The characters of TodaysGirls.com chat online in the safest—and maybe most fun—of all chat rooms! They've created their own private Web site and room! Many Christian teen sites allow you to create your own private chat rooms, and there are other safe options.

Work with your parents to develop a list of safe, appropriate chat rooms. Earn Internet freedom by showing them you can make the right choices. *Honor your father and your mother (Deuteronomy 5:16).*

Before entering a chat room, you'll select a user name. Although you can use your real name, a nickname is safer. Most people choose one that says something about who they are, like Amber's name, faithful1. Don't be discouraged if the name you select is already taken. You can use a similar one by adding a number at its end.

No one will notice your grammar in a chat room. Don't worry if you spell something wrong or forget to capitalize. Some people even misspell words on purpose. You might see a sentence like How R U?

But sometimes it's important to be accurate. Web site and e-mail addresses must be exact. Pay close attention to whether letters are upper- or lowercase. Remember that Web site addresses don't use some punctuation marks, such as hyphens and apostrophes. (That's why the "Today's" in TodaysGirls.com has no apostrophe!) And instead of using spaces between words, underlines are used to_make_the_spaces. And sometimes words just run together like onebigword.

When you're in a chat room, remember that real people are typing the words that appear on your screen. Treat them with the same respect you expect from them. Don't say anything you wouldn't want repeated in Sunday school. *Do for other people what you want them to do for you (Luke 6:31).*

Sometimes people say mean, hurtful things—things that make us angry. This can happen in chat rooms, too. In some chat rooms, you can highlight a rude person's name and click a button that says, "ignore," which will make his or her comments disappear from your screen. You always have the option to switch rooms or sign off. If a particular person becomes a continual problem, or if someone says something especially vicious, you should report this problem user to the chat service. *Ask God to bless those who say bad things to you. Pray for those who are cruel (Luke 6:28–29).*

Remember that Internet information is not always factual. Whether you're chatting or surfing Web sites, be skeptical about information and people. Not everything on the Internet is true. You don't have to be afraid of the Internet, but you should always be cautious. Practice caution with others even in Christian chat rooms.

It's okay to chat about your likes and dislikes, but *never* give out personal information. Do not tell anyone your name, phone number, address, or even the name of your school, team, church, or neighborhood. Be cautious . . . *You will be like sheep among wolves. So be as smart as snakes. But also be like doves and do nothing wrong. Be careful of people (Matthew 10:16–17).*

Cyber Glossary

Bounced mail An e-mail that has been returned to its sender.

Chat A live conversation, typed or spoken through microphones, among individuals in a chat room.

Chat room A "place" on the Internet where individuals meet to "talk" with one another.

Crack To break a security code.

Download To receive information from a more powerful computer.

E-mail Electronic mail that is sent through the Internet.

E-mail address An Internet address where e-mail is received.

File Any document or image stored on a computer.

Floppy disk A small, thin, plastic object that stores information to be accessed by a computer.

Hacker Someone who tries to gain unauthorized access to another computer or network of computers.

Header Text at the beginning of an e-mail that identifies the sender, subject matter, and the time at which it was sent.

Home page A Web site's first page.

Internet A worldwide electronic network that connects computers to one another.

Link Highlighted text or a graphic element that may be clicked with the mouse in order to "surf" to another Web site or page.

Log on/Log in To connect to a computer network.

Modem A device that enables computers to exchange information.

Net, the The Internet.

Newbie A person who is learning or participating in something new.

Online To have Internet access. Can also mean to use the Internet.

Surf To move from page to page through links on the Web.

Upload To send information to a more powerful computer.

Web, the The World Wide Web or WWW.